THE LAKE PALACE

ANN BENNETT

Andaman Press

For Talei, in memory of our travels.

1

As the train swayed and bumped through the night across the great plain towards Ranipur, Iris leaned out of her bunk, lifted the frayed curtain and peered through the open window. It seemed as though the whole country was blanketed in darkness and it was difficult to see anything, other than twinkling pinpricks of light marking distant villages.

Occasionally, with much clattering and clanging of bells, the train rumbled over a level crossing. Iris would catch a glimpse of a dimly lit village street, lorries and motor-rickshaws lined up waiting for the train to pass, pedestrians waiting by the gate, their patient faces lit up by lamplight.

Iris returned to lying on her back, staring at the light flickering on the ceiling, unable to sleep, despite the soporific swaying of the train; there was far too much to think about.

It was magical to be back in India after almost forty years. Just lying there, imagining the vast plain they were travelling across, smelling the woodsmoke from village fires on the warm night air, brought the memories flooding back. She felt so at home here, how could she have been away for so long? And now she *was* back, it was almost as if she'd never left. She sighed. It was difficult to enthuse about India too much with Elspeth as her travelling companion. Iris hated to admit it to herself, but she knew now that it would have been far easier and far more congenial if she'd had the courage to make the journey alone. Even now, above the rattle of the wheels on the track, the sound of loud, persistent snoring floated up from the lower bunk, a constant reminder of her companion. Iris smiled to herself. Elspeth was so proper, so convinced of her own superiority, Iris hadn't dared mention the snoring, but it secretly amused her nonetheless.

Iris shuddered, as the numerous embarrassments Elspeth had caused on their trip came back to her. There had been several toe-curling moments already, even though they'd only been in India ten days or so. Iris realised that she should have known how Elspeth would react to her surroundings; after all, why would she have changed dramatically from how she'd been as a young woman? But the truth was, the passage of time had softened Iris' memories and removed some of the rough edges and troublesome traits from people she'd known back then.

It was clear from the moment they stepped off the plane at Indira Gandhi Airport in Delhi that Elspeth wasn't going to find India to her liking. Firstly, there was the waiter at the hotel, whom Elspeth had chided for not addressing her as madam.

'Let me tell you, young man,' she'd said, peering at him over her pince-nez as he poured her breakfast tea, 'In my father's day, you would have known to mind your Ps and Qs. My father would not tolerate rudeness or insubordination. Not from anyone.'

'Elspeth, really!' Iris had hissed, her eyes fixed on the table, shrivelling inside with humiliation. Elspeth ignored her protests, but as Iris looked up she caught the waiter's eye. He smiled conspiratorially at her and raised an eyebrow. She'd looked away quickly, hoping that Elspeth hadn't noticed the exchange.

'This generation. Honestly!' Elspeth had muttered as the waiter walked away.

'I don't think it's a good idea to mention British rule, Elspeth,' Iris had whispered, leaning forward. 'They have left it behind and they don't want to be reminded. Especially the young people.'

Elspeth had fixed her with a cold, hard stare. 'Things were much better in this country back then. Surely even you can see that, Iris? Standards have slipped dreadfully.'

But Iris didn't agree. She'd been more than happy with her simple room in the hotel off Connaught Place in Delhi, and had not found anything to complain about. She'd been delighted with the feel of the cool marble tiles under her bare feet, the crisp linen sheets on the bed, lying awake watching the spindly ceiling fan whirring on its axis, listening to the horns of the motor rickshaws. In contrast, Elspeth had complained about everything; her toilet didn't flush properly, there was a lizard on the bathroom wall, there was no air-conditioning and the room was noisy.

Anyone would think she'd never been to India before, Iris had thought to herself as she stood twisting her hands helplessly while Elspeth berated the bemused man on the reception desk about the shortcomings of the hotel. *She grew up here. Surely, she can remember that lizards on the bathroom wall are a fact of life?*

'And I'll need a room on the ground floor,' Elspeth finished her diatribe. 'I can't possibly be expected to get up and down that awkward staircase with my poorly leg.' She waved her walking stick at the man, who bowed his head.

'I'm very sorry, madam,' he said. 'Not to worry. We will provide you with ground floor room without delay.'

Iris secretly wondered what was actually wrong with Elspeth's leg. She'd never dared ask. She and Elspeth were both in their early sixties, but where Iris was lithe and active, only a few grey hairs and lines on her face belying her years, Elspeth had already embraced old age with gusto. She was running to fat and the years showed in her face and in the way she moved. She leaned heavily on her stick when she walked. Her stick and her bad leg were two immutable facts and something told Iris it would have been unthinkable to enquire about them.

Then there had been the old rickshaw-wallah in Agra, who had generously offered Elspeth a blanket to keep her warm in the chilly morning air as he'd pedalled them through the wakening streets to watch the sun rise over the Taj Mahal. Elspeth had flinched and pushed the blanket away, shaking her head vehemently. 'No, thank you. I don't want to start itching,' she'd said, frowning.

'Oh, Elspeth,' Iris had said, seeing the man's crestfallen expression. Elspeth had harumphed noisily in the seat next to her. Iris had hoped desperately that the man hadn't understood.

Everywhere they went, Elspeth seemed to relish the fuss and attention that her leg and her stick afforded her. Bearers hovered round her in hotels, anxious to take her bags, to find her somewhere to sit; rickshaw wallahs would climb down from their cycles and help her up into the seat; the best tables were offered at restaurants, guards on trains helped her into carriages. But still she wasn't happy. Mopping her brow constantly, batting away insects and holding a handkerchief over her nose against the street smells, it seemed to Iris that Elspeth must have completely forgotten about India during her years in England.

'Dear Lord, the noise, Iris. However can you stand it?' Elspeth had shouted when they were halfway down Chandni Chowk in the Old Town in Delhi. Iris had managed to persuade her to visit the street market one evening and was revelling in the sights and sounds, the vibrant colours and the clamour of the street vendors, the smell of cooking spices on the evening air. At that point she was bargaining with a tenacious salesman over a length of aquamarine silk. She had no particular use for it, but she loved the colour so much she just had to have it. She turned to look at Elspeth, surprised at her words. Elspeth's grey curls were plastered to her forehead, her blouse was sticking to her skin and she held a handkerchief over her mouth. Iris had a vision then of how Elspeth had been in her youth in the 1940s, one of the club set, in a floral dress and bright red lipstick, sipping stengahs at the bar, laughing and joking with the other club bores. She realised then that the India Elspeth had inhabited as a young woman wasn't the one Iris herself had known. Elspeth had confined herself to the club, to her father's spacious bungalow with its large garden and deep veranda, to tea parties, and to watching polo matches on the maiden from the shade of a tent. Unlike Iris, she must never have explored the bazaars and markets of the old town, travelled into the countryside to seek out overgrown temples or deserted palaces. In that moment, Iris realised what a mistake it had been to decide to travel back here with Elspeth.

It had happened quite by chance. Doreen Mulligan, a mutual friend, who'd also lived in India in the forties, had brought them together. Iris had been sitting alone in her kitchen one gloomy afternoon, staring out at the frost-covered garden. She was grieving for her husband, Andrew, who'd died suddenly that January. Iris had found it difficult to accept. After thirty-five years of marriage, it was like losing part of herself and she felt at sea. Doreen had brought her flowers that day and had sat down at the table opposite her, peering at her with concern.

'You need something to cheer you up, Iris,' Doreen had pronounced. 'You're not yourself. A holiday, maybe?'

'Oh, I wouldn't know where to go. I've not been away by myself since I got married,' she'd murmured listlessly. It was true. There was nowhere that appealed to her.

'Why don't you go and stay with Caroline or Pete?'

Iris shook her head. Her son and daughter were both occupied with their own young families, with their busy careers. Although she loved them both dearly and they would have welcomed her, somehow it wouldn't have felt like a holiday.

'Well...is there anywhere you've dreamed about visiting? Always wanted to go but never got round to it?'

There was only one place she ever dreamed of and that was somewhere she would never, ever have suggested visiting to Andrew. It belonged to her alone, existed only in *her* memory, and over the years had taken on an almost mystical quality in her mind; the lake at Nagabhari and its palace built on an island, but seeming to float on the surface, with its domes and cupolas, shimmering white in the morning mist. The little town on the edge of the lake with its bustling market place and small British quarter where she'd lived in that tight-knit community with her parents. That's the place she'd dreamed about for forty years. She'd tried to put it all behind her; it held too many painful memories and associations, and until that moment she'd never contemplated actually returning.

'What about India?' Doreen had said suddenly.

Iris blinked. Could Doreen actually see it in her eyes? That sad, lonely longing of hers?

'What on earth made you think of India?' she asked.

'Well, I was going to mention this before. You remember Elspeth James? We exchange Christmas cards and vaguely keep in touch. Sadly, her husband also died last year and she happened to mention to me that she was thinking of taking a trip back there, only she didn't want to go alone. She asked me if I'd like to go.'

'And would you?'

Doreen shook her head. 'I'm far too busy, with my volunteering and the grandchildren. And besides, George would never go and he'd never want me to go away for long without him.'

Iris swallowed.

'Oh, I'm sorry, darling,' Doreen slid her hand over hers on the table. 'That was very tactless of me. But... well, why don't you give it some thought. I've got Elspeth's number. It might be good for both of you to catch up anyway.'

Iris tried to picture Elspeth and all she could conjure was the image of her in the club, the one that kept returning to her on the trip. They had never been close back in the forties, but perhaps they would have more in common now. Elspeth's father had been the commanding officer at Army HQ in Nagabhari, and Iris' own father was the British Resident of Ranipur, the British government's representative in the princely state. Their mothers were best friends though, Josie and Delphine, virtually inseparable. Always visiting each other in the afternoons for bridge or tiffin, sitting together on the club veranda with their cigarette holders and gin and tonics in the afternoon, their elegant heads bent together in endless gossip.

Iris had met Elspeth for an afternoon in London and despite some niggling misgivings, allowed herself to be persuaded into booking the trip. They would do the tourist sights of Delhi, Agra, Jaipur and Benares, before taking the sleeper train east to Ranipur, which lay on the border with Burma. Now, lying on the bunk, trying to sleep, Iris wondered what Elspeth's motivation for the trip was. It was clear that she wasn't enjoying the country and only occasionally, when they'd been exploring the Pink City of Jaipur, or wandering through the marbled halls of the Taj Mahal had she seen Elspeth relax enough to smile at the beauty of their surroundings. She concluded it must have been boredom and nostalgia for her youth and for the good old days of the Raj that had brought Elspeth back.

Perhaps it was a hankering for a time when she and her family had been in a position of wealth and power, but judging by what Elspeth had told Iris about her husband's wealth and success and her privileged life in England, there would seem to be no need for that. Elspeth clearly thought she was a cut above Iris – her husband had been the managing director of an engineering firm and she'd never worked in her life. She had made a couple of disparaging remarks about the fact that Iris had had her own career as a teacher when she'd returned to England after the war.

Iris wondered fleetingly whether Elspeth had a reason as compelling as her own to return to the place where they'd spent their early twenties. For many years, Iris had put those memories behind her. She'd settled down in England and lived happily with Andrew and their children. It was almost as if it was a different life and as if those momentous, magical but also painful events had never happened to her. She'd kept them shut away in a vault in the deepest recesses of her mind, but now the vault was open and those memories were flooding back, threatening to overwhelm her with their impact and their potency.

She sat up suddenly, switched on the reading light and reached for the knapsack she'd wedged at the bottom of the bunk. She'd been putting it off, but now the time was right. Rummaging amongst the detritus of travel; the pens and tissues, mosquito repellent and sunglasses, she pulled out the little hardback, mottled-blue exercise book that she'd written in religiously throughout that tumultuous time that had changed her life for ever. It had not been opened for forty years and the pages were stiff, some stuck together. She held it in her hands, staring at the cover, afraid to open up that Pandora's box of the past. And even as she did so, the lights in the carriage flickered and went out. She sighed and slipped the book back into her knapsack and snuggled down under the blanket. She could have found her torch, but perhaps the power failure was telling her something. Perhaps it would be better to wait until they reached Nagabhari after all. She closed her eyes and finally the gentle swaying of the train sent her off to sleep.

2

Nagabhari, India, 1985

A steward had taken their order for breakfast when they'd first boarded the train in Benares, explaining that it would be telegraphed ahead to another station down the line. And sure enough, several hundred miles down the track and sixteen hours later, a young boy with bare feet brought it on a tray to their compartment. It was just after dawn and the bunks had already been stripped and stowed away by the steward. Iris sat beside Elspeth on the bench seat while the boy assembled the collapsible table and laid out their food on china plates. Iris had asked for an Indian meal of dosa and curry, while Elspeth had ordered English breakfast; porridge and omelette.

'I don't know how you can eat that spicy food so early in the morning,' Elspeth grumbled with a shudder. 'It would turn my stomach.'

Iris shrugged and smiled, biting into the deliciously crispy dosa. 'It's what the locals eat.'

'Yes, well, we're not locals.'

'I *was* born in India, Elspeth,' Iris laughed, eyeing the rubbery looking omelette and dried up toast on Elspeth's plate. 'You were too, weren't you?'

Elspeth paused, a slice of toast halfway to her mouth. 'Well, if you count the British hospital in Simla as India, I suppose I was, technically. But there is a difference. As you well know.'

Iris smiled, wondering at the fine distinctions Elspeth made in her mind to bolster her entrenched opinions and sense of entitlement.

'We always ate Indian breakfast at home when we lived here,' she told Elspeth a little mischievously. 'Mother preferred it.'

'Well, that figures,' Elspeth replied with a knowing look. Iris wondered what she meant and was about to ask her when she noticed that they were passing through a small station – the signs on the platform showing it to be the town of Pripura.

'Oh look, we must be in Ranipur state already! It can only be a few miles to Nagabhari now. We'd better eat up.'

'I don't suppose we need to hurry. At the rate this train travels, we won't be there until lunchtime.'

Ignoring Elspeth's gloomy predictions, Iris gave her full attention to her dosa, which oozed with succulent flavours, and stared out of the window at the unfolding landscape. Now clear of the little town, they were rolling through lush fields where animals grazed, past villages and farmsteads, no more than a few huts grouped together under palm trees, they clattered over iron bridges above muddy rivers and past ponds where buffalo wallowed. The sky was tinged with a pink glow and the rising sun shimmered in the morning mist. Iris was tingling with excitement now at the prospect of being back in Nagabhari, but she was full of uncertainties too. What would the town be like now? Would she still recognise the place?

What about her old home? And would anyone still live here who might remember her? She suddenly had a panicked thought. Was it madness to come back after all this time? Whatever good would it do her to dig up the past?

The train chugged on towards Nagabhari, and Iris, glued to the window now, began to recognise various features of the landscape; a deserted temple, a couple of small lakes where water birds waded and early morning fishermen cast their nets from little boats. Then, lifting her gaze, she noticed a grey smudge on the landscape which must be the Naga Hills – the mountain range that bordered Burma. Just the sight of them made her heart lurch – so much had happened to her in those distant hills during the war.

'Nagabhari – only ten minutes now, madam,' the guard announced passing their compartment. Elspeth began an elaborate manoeuvre to retrieve her case from under the seat.

'Here, let me help you with that,' Iris said, crouching down and pulling both cases out.

'Don't you do that, Iris. There is bound to be a porter at the station to carry our luggage. They can come on board and take them. Ask the guard.'

'I can at least get the cases to the door,' said Iris briskly, heaving them out of the compartment and into the corridor while Elspeth fussed around with her stick.

At last, the train bumped and jolted to a halt and someone opened the carriage door. A group of porters swarmed around the steps clamouring for trade as Iris climbed down. She quickly picked the strongest-looking man, handed him both cases then turned back to help Elspeth down from the train. As their luggage was borne out of the station on the porter's head, Iris took a moment to absorb her surroundings. The past came back to her in a rush. The station was just as she remembered it. The signs were modern, but apart from looking a little shabbier, lacking the neat pot plants and needing a lick of paint, the red-brick Victorian building had hardly changed since she had last stood on this spot. She'd been a young woman then and it seemed a lifetime ago when she'd come to the station to board a train bound for New Delhi with her parents in 1944.

They followed the porter through the station building that was already crowded with people waiting for trains, some sleeping on the benches, others squatting on the floor in groups with parcels and boxes. The heat of the morning sun hit them as they stepped out of the shade of the building and onto the forecourt. The porter had already engaged a motor-rickshaw and their luggage was stowed on the shelf behind the seat.

'Lake View Hotel, driver,' Elspeth commanded as the driver helped her into her seat. They had gleaned, before leaving the UK, that the old British Club where Elspeth had spent so much time in her youth had been converted into a small hotel and it had seemed the obvious place to stay. Iris had worried, given what Elspeth had said about her husband's successful business, that their budgets would be very different. She herself, on her teacher's pension and with the little money that Andrew had left her, had to be very careful. But strangely it turned out that Elspeth was on an even tighter budget than she was and was quite prepared to stay in lowly guesthouses and cheap hotels, although it clearly rankled with her.

With a blast of the horn, the rickshaw-wallah pulled out into the stream of traffic and began to drive them through the chaotic streets of downtown Nagabhari. To Iris, clinging onto a strap, it seemed very busy. She'd got used to the noisy, turbulent roads in Delhi, but she'd been expecting Nagabhari to be the sleepy little place that occupied her memory. Instead, there was the usual confusion of bicycles, rickshaws, taxis and assorted trucks, not to mention pony tongas and bullock carts jostling for space in the narrow streets. She strained to recognise anything. Some of the buildings along the main street must have been there in her youth, but many were crumbling and dilapidated, with vegetation growing from gutters and parapets and were barely recognisable now.

They crawled through the centre of the old town, breathing in neat petrol fumes that belted out from dilapidated buses. A street market was in full swing, spilling out and down the steps of the old building that housed a covered market. Iris' gaze was drawn to the scene – the colourful stalls stacked with all kinds of produce, women in bright sarees bargaining for fruit and vegetables, food vendors cooking on open fires, a chai-wallah parading with a large kettle, hawking his wares at the top of his voice.

'This heat is unbearable,' Elspeth complained, fanning herself furiously with a book, but Iris didn't reply. Just looking at that scene had broken a memory from 1944 when she'd visited that market. She'd been showing someone the sights of Nagabhari and had taken him there to experience some local colour. She bit her lip, remembering that bitter-sweet interlude. Of course, it wasn't just *someone*. She realised then, staring into the recesses of the bustling market, that those few days had made a bigger impact on her life than almost anything else either before or since, and it was the tug of that time that had finally brought her back here. But as she stared at the scene, the rickshaw moved on, leaving the market behind.

Soon they were out of the town centre and heading towards the lake. The roads were quieter here, the buildings further apart. At a crossroads, Iris noticed a signpost to Nagabhari University and she instantly thought of Sharmila. The beautiful, troubled Indian girl, the wife of one of the lecturers, who'd become her friend and confidante. Did Sharmila still live along that tree-lined road in the shady bungalow she'd shared with her husband? Were they still together after everything that had happened? Guilt stirred inside Iris. They had vowed to write when she left, but their correspondence had dwindled away to nothing after a few years; work and marriage and children had taken over. During those busy years, her life in India had seemed faraway, like a dream existence that might well never have happened.

'Oh, look,' Elspeth's voice broke into her thoughts. 'There's our old house,' but her bright tone quickly turned to disappointment. 'Oh, no, just *look* at it!'

The once proud bungalow with its pillars, deep verandas and gardens that had been immaculate, filled with canna lilies and geraniums, looked very run down now. A couple of lorries were parked up in the front drive and the place had all the hallmarks of the headquarters of some sort of haulage business. Iris felt a twinge of pity for Elspeth, but in the next road they passed Iris' own home which had fared even worse down the years. Like Elspeth's it was neglected and crumbling away, but Iris' house appeared to be abandoned, with wire netting over the windows and goats grazing in the overgrown front garden. Iris felt a pang of sorrow for the place she'd spent so many happy years, but she wasn't surprised. It just brought home to her the changes wrought by the passage of time.

Swinging into the entrance of the old club, the sight of the familiar building took Iris' breath away. There it stood as it always had, nestled amongst rose beds and ornamental palms, with its green shutters, white pillars and sweeping verandas; it had been restored to its former glory. Apart from the painted sign above the entrance which proclaimed "Lake View Hotel" they could have been transported back forty years.

For the first time since they'd arrived, Iris noticed a

genuine smile spread across Elspeth's face as they clambered out of the motor-rickshaw. Inside the shaded entrance hall, cooled by whirring fans, a reception desk stood in the corner where the old chowkidar, the caretaker, used to sit, but apart from that, nothing had changed. The same hunting prints were still on the walls, a stuffed tiger's head hung above the mantlepiece, and the place even smelt the same; of leather, polish and cigars.

'Would you like a room on the ground floor, madam?' asked the man on reception, noticing Elspeth's stick. Elspeth positively glowed with pleasure.

The rooms they were given were side by side at the end of the corridor and both had double doors opening onto private verandas with a view of the lake. Once inside her room, having tipped the hotel bearer who'd brought the luggage, Iris heaved a grateful sigh to be alone at last. She was tired enough to flop down on the bed, but the urge to see the lake was strong. She went straight to the double doors, out onto the veranda and leaned on the balustrade taking in deep breaths of the hot, moist air. There it was, stretching out in front of her. The huge, magical lake that had occupied her memory for forty years, as enigmatic and beautiful today as it ever had been. And there, far in the distance, on the other side was the majestic palace. It still seemed to float on the water, shimmering in the mist as it always had. Iris had read in her guide book that the palace was no longer occupied, that the maharajah and his family had left after Independence to live a nomadic life in their various residences across Europe and the Middle East. The old palace was a museum now, open to the public on certain days. That saddened her, but she couldn't wait to go there, to walk those marbled corridors once again and remember how it once had been.

They ate lunch in the high-ceilinged dining room,

furnished with potted palms and oak furniture. There were few other guests and only one of the other tables was occupied – a young couple from Germany.

'Shall we visit the Lake Palace this afternoon?' Iris asked tentatively. She knew they were both tired and it might be more sensible to wait until the next day, but she couldn't wait. To her surprise, Elspeth agreed. 'Why not? No time like the present.'

A group of rickshaws waited under the banyan trees that shaded the club entrance, their owners reclining on the seats, resting from the heat of the early afternoon, but when Iris came out onto the steps, one of them sat up immediately and came over to speak to her. They quickly negotiated a price for him to take her and Elspeth to the ghat where boats departed for the palace. There was the usual fuss as Elspeth got up into the rickshaw, but once they were on their way, bumping along the rough track that ran alongside the lake, Iris' excitement began to mount.

It only took a few minutes to get to the pontoon, where public boats departed for the palace every hour, but there were private boats moored up there too. Iris haggled with one of the boatmen who agreed to take just the two of them. Both the rickshaw-wallah and the boatman helped Elspeth down into the boat, each taking an arm and she sat awkwardly on the bench, under a sunshade, her bad leg stretched out in front of her.

All the fuss was quickly forgotten when the boat finally pulled away from the pontoon and set off across the lake towards the palace; the chug-chug of the engine the only sound on the still water. The boatman lit a cheroot and Elspeth waved the smoke away pointedly, but Iris rather liked the smell of the rough tobacco. It took her back.

She trailed her hand in the cool water as they moved

across the surface of the lake, the shimmering white palace dominating the horizon. As they got closer, she could make out individual domes and towers.

Elspeth kept up an incessant chatter: 'I expect this brings back memories for you, Iris. Do you remember coming across here for functions in the old days? Oh, the maharajah's parties were quite magnificent, weren't they?'

But Iris didn't reply. She just wanted to absorb the atmosphere. How many times had she crossed the lake in a boat with her father, accompanying him on his official trips to the palace? He would go to brief the maharajah almost daily, being the political agent, the representative of the British government in Ranipur state, and she would beg him to take her too, when she was young. She loved visiting the palace, the endless echoing marble chambers, the royal women in their brightly coloured silks and, if she was lucky, one of the princesses would take her by the hand and show her the secret nooks and crannies of the place and invite her to play with them in one of the many courtyards.

They drew closer and it became apparent that although the palace still looked the same from a distance, it was no longer the pristine building it had once been. White paint was peeling from its domes and arches, revealing the grey stone underneath, and the lower walls were covered with green algae. Close up, it looked a little forlorn, Iris noted with a pang.

At last the boat arrived at the little landing stage under the palace walls. The boatman tied up to the jetty, then jumped ashore and held out his hand for Elspeth to take. The boat wobbled dangerously as the boatman and Iris helped Elspeth to climb out, then Iris followed her. She stood there on the jetty, in front of the steps she'd mounted so many times before, now decaying with age and neglect, her heart pounding with anticipation.

'Come on, Elspeth. I'll help you.' She took Elspeth's arm and they went up the steps together. At the top, they arrived at a marble walkway bordered with delicately latticed marble walls, which led to the arched entrance to the palace. Elspeth stopped, mopping her brow with a handkerchief.

'You go on and explore, Iris. I think I'll just sit down here in the breeze and catch my breath.'

'I can wait with you...' she offered, but Elspeth shook her head.

'No. You go on. I'll follow you in a bit.'

'All right then, if you're sure.'

Iris turned left along the walkway and soon found herself in one of the many ornamental walled gardens. She'd expected it to be neglected and overgrown, judging by the state of the building, but the flowerbeds between box hedges were neat and the lawn was still pristine, surrounded by palm trees swaying in the breeze from the lake. She walked slowly on through the garden. She'd been here many times before and the feeling was so familiar. Stepping through an archway, she found herself standing on a hexagonal marble platform that jutted out above the lake. It had been built like that to catch the evening breezes. There was a domed ceiling and the eight arched openings that looked out over the lake were filled with latticed marble. She stood in the centre of the tower, letting the chills of recognition go right through her. The years melted away and she was transported back in time, to that warm evening early in 1944 when she'd stood in that very spot. It was the evening of the maharajah's dinner, when she'd come out here to get some air – that fateful evening, when she had first met Edward Stark.

3

Nagabhari, India, January, 1944

Iris straightened up and wiped her brow with the back of her hand. She cast a nervous glance around the overcrowded ward. It was filled with wounded men, stretched out on the beds in bloody uniforms, some writhing in pain, some lying worryingly still. Nurses and doctors moved quickly from bed to bed, trying to attend to those with the worst injuries, but it was an impossible task. Iris had been shocked when she'd arrived for her usual shift that morning. Until that point there had only been a trickle of wounded soldiers coming down to the city hospital in Nagabhari from skirmishes with the Japanese in the Naga Hills. The British and Indian Armies were stationed there to prevent a Japanese invasion of British India. But today when she'd arrived, a column of army trucks was parked up outside. And as she entered, the corridors were filled with wounded men lying on stretchers, on makeshift beds, some even stretched out on the floor. The sickly smell of blood filled the air.

'Bring this man some water, quickly, nurse,' a doctor

called, and she snapped to attention and pushed her trolley quickly between the beds to where the doctor was examining one of the soldiers. The man's face was deathly pale and sheened with sweat, he appeared semi-conscious and unable to focus, his pupils disappearing up into his eyelids. With a shock, she noticed that one of his shins had been shattered, fragments of bone stuck out through torn, blood-stained trousers. Trying not to look at the wound, Iris quickly poured a cup of water and held it to the man's lips. He took in a few drops, but a lot dribbled down his chin.

'Try again, nurse,' said the doctor. 'He's badly dehydrated.'

'What happened, do you know?' she asked, as she held the cup up to those dry, peeling lips again. The doctor shook his head. 'Not much. The Japs have mounted a new offensive. We weren't prepared for them. That's all I know.'

'It's terrible,' she whispered, her eyes on the soldier in the bed. He could only be nineteen or twenty, younger even than Iris herself. All the men lying in the ward were around the same age. Some Indian, some British. Her heart went out to those young boys, so far from home, completely unprepared for the harsh conditions of jungle warfare and the fierce opponent they would face there.

She'd been helping out at the hospital for several months. Her father had suggested it, noticing how bored and restless she'd become at home. She'd been back in India for three years now, since finishing boarding school and secretarial studies in London, and had been at a loose end ever since. Until the war came to the nearby hills and the city hospital suddenly needed volunteers to help with the extra work.

Although she loved India – she'd been born on the subcontinent and lived here until she was sent to school in England aged eleven – she found life in the small British community in the princely state of Ranipur deadly dull.

Evenings at the club drinking and playing bridge were not for her. Instead, she loved to explore the countryside on horseback, or to wander about in the old town, losing herself in the deep alleyways and colourful bazaars, but she felt very alone. Since returning to India, she'd had a restlessness about her that she found hard to tame. The problem was, she had no idea what she was looking for.

She'd hoped that her father would take her with him to the palace sometimes, as he used to when she was small, but things had got very tense in Ranipur state lately and he'd explained that it would no longer be possible. Besides, the prince and princesses she used to play with as a child no longer lived at home. The girls had been married off to princes from other parts of India, and Ranjit, the maharajah's only son, was away in London. The maharajah was having a difficult time, facing rioting and rebellions from his subjects on many fronts and Iris' father had his hands full helping him cope.

'Do carry on, nurse,' said the doctor, 'All the men in this ward are in need of water,' and he moved along to the next patient.

Iris watched the young doctor. He was tall and angular, with soft, pale skin, light brown hair and a blushing complexion. He'd tried to open a conversation with her more than once as she'd sat sipping tea and smoking in the canteen during her morning breaks, but he was so nervous that he couldn't meet her eye and she quickly ran out of things to say to him. Deep down, she could tell he was well meaning and kind, but nothing could overcome the fact that she also found him awkward and dreadfully dull. She felt a little sorry for him, out here in India all alone, with only the club as an outlet. She'd seen him there once or twice, drinking at the bar alone, watching nervously from the sidelines as the cliquey club crowd got drunk and raucous together, too shy to open a conversation with anyone. Not that it would have been easy, even for the most hardened, outgoing person. Like her, he clearly didn't fit in there, but probably for different reasons.

She carried on going from bed to bed, offering water to the injured men. Some could barely speak, some were shaking so much, or so weak that they couldn't hold the cup to their lips so she had to do it for them. Each time she saw the gratitude in their eyes. One, with a bloody bandage round his head, had been so rattled by his experience on the battlefield that he couldn't stop talking. As Iris neared his bed and offered him water, he clearly saw her as someone to engage in conversation.

'Bloody wily enemy, the Jap, nurse,' he said as he took the cup from her. 'Surrounded us on the ridge, they did. They'd somehow managed to circle round behind us and they came out of the trees at us from every direction. Brutal they were. Fearless. Ran at us yelling blue murder, with bayonets pointing. Every man in my unit was struck down. Dead most of 'em...'

'Shut up, Pete,' groaned his neighbour. 'We know. You've told us a thousand times.'

As Iris progressed around the ward, she picked up many similar snippets of information from the men; they'd been on a routine patrol in the hills when they were ambushed and attacked by the Japanese.

'Bad planning, I'd call it,' said one man.

'Shut up. You know we're not meant to talk about it.'

In the afternoon, the ward sister asked Iris to accompany her on her rounds to dress wounds. It took all her strength and resolve to remain calm and not to look away or to faint, as she helped sister clean the dirt and pus from shattered limbs, head wounds, stomach wounds, wounds of every size, shape and description. Many of the men were not just injured. They were also very thin, their bellies bloated, their arms and legs like sticks. They were pale too and many were suffering from some sort of tropical disease. All had many swollen insect bites and were covered in little red wounds where leeches had burrowed into their skin. Sometimes the black, bloated leeches were still there, sucking the blood. Iris recoiled at the sight of them, but sister would light a match and burn them off.

'It's the only way. If you pull them off, the teeth stay in the skin and you quickly get blood poisoning.'

By the end of the day most of the soldiers in the ward had been tended to. Two had died and had been hastily covered with a sheet and stretchered out by the hospital porters with the minimum of fuss.

'You should go now,' the sister told her, glancing at her watch. The sky was rapidly growing dark outside. 'You've stayed far longer than your normal hours. Thank you so much, nurse.'

The sister, a little Irish woman with dark hair, had rings of exhaustion under her eyes.

'I could stay, sister. You look very tired yourself.'

'I won't be long. You get off, nurse. Thank you again for your help today.'

Iris left the ward and changed into trousers and a blouse in the cloakroom. She felt drained, dead on her feet, but she didn't want to go home. Daddy would be buried in paperwork in his study as usual. She had no desire to go to the club either; Elspeth and her crowd were always there. Iris loathed their boorish behaviour and predictable conversation. And Mother would be there too, drinking and smoking the night away, gossiping and giggling with her friend, Josie. They would both be dressed up to the nines, seeking any male attention that was on offer. Poor Daddy.

Instead, she got onto her bike which she'd left outside the hospital entrance, and cycled out through the town centre, glad to be breathing the fresh air at last, free of the stuffy ward. She cycled through the busy streets of the shopping district, still lit up and thronging with street life. She was making for the well-tended bungalows and leafy gardens that surrounded the university. Halfway along that road, she pulled into the driveway of one of the smaller residences, seeing lights through the cracks in the shutters, and leaned her bike against the porch.

A servant came to the door at her knock. She was just enquiring if the lady of the house was at home when behind him in the hallway she caught sight of Sharmila, hovering. Iris was shocked to see that the kohl from her eyes had smudged down her cheeks. She'd been crying, but as soon as she saw Iris her eyes lit up. She stepped forward.

'I'm so glad you've come, Iris! You haven't been for days. Come on in.'

'Are you alone?'

Sharmila nodded and Iris followed her through into the small front room, where they both sunk down on the big silk cushions scattered around the floor.

'Deepak is still out, I'm afraid,' Iris caught anxiety in Sharmila's tone, but she went on; 'He has a lot of work on at the moment. Building up to examinations.'

'Of course.'

'So, I'm not worried. He is often late.'

'I understand.'

'Would you like anything to drink? Fruit juice? Tea?'

'Tea would be wonderful. It's been a busy day.'

Sharmila got to her feet and went into the hall to speak to the servant.

'You look tired, Iris,' Sharmila said, sitting back down beside Iris. 'Have you been at the hospital?'

Iris nodded and told Sharmila all about the sudden influx of casualties from the front.

'It's never happened before. Not like today anyway. Things are definitely heating up, up there in the hills.'

Fresh anxiety entered Sharmila's gaze. 'Yes. It is a worry,' she said, her brows knitted, 'Father is worried about a Japanese invasion.'

'Everyone is, but not many people are prepared to speak about it. But you know, many Indians would welcome it.'

'Oh no, Iris. Please do not say so.'

'Well, surely you know about the Indian National Army? Lots of Indian soldiers have defected from the British Indian Army to fight in it. They, like others, are prepared to fight to get the British out of India.'

Sharmila lowered her eyes. 'Some, yes. But not me,' she said quietly. 'And not my father either. He says the Japanese would be far, far worse rulers than the British.'

Iris smiled. 'What about Deepak?' she asked gently. 'What does he say?'

Sharmila shook her head, an expression of despair on her face. 'I don't ask anymore. It's best not to. I hope his days of protest are behind him now. But... but...'

'But what, Sharmila?'

'I worry, that's all. After what happened before.'

They both fell silent. Iris was remembering what Sharmila had told her about how Deepak had come here to Nagabhari. He was a talented academic, with a first-class degree in English, but he'd arrived at the university under a cloud. He'd been employed at Ganpur and Benares universities before.

Some of the details of what had happened in Ganpur were shrouded in mystery, but Sharmila had a better idea about Benares, although the details of that were still hazy. She knew that he'd become radicalised, although she had no idea why, and that he had become an embarrassment to the faculty. He'd only found a post at Nagabhari because Sharmila's father, Professor Ramesh, the head of the English faculty there, had taken him under his wing, recognising his talent, and had fought his cause.

The servant came in, clearing his throat loudly, with a silver tray of tea things. He put it down on the low table between them and left the room. Sharmila poured tea for both of them, her face still clouded with worry.

'That was then, Sharmila,' Iris said. 'Things have changed for Deepak now, haven't they?'

'I suppose so,' Sharmila replied, biting her nail.

Iris wondered what she could say to cheer her friend up. Perhaps she shouldn't have mentioned the war and the unrest, it had clearly unsettled Sharmila. She worried about her friend. Sharmila had told her how she'd fallen in love with Deepak the first time she'd met him, and Iris had to admit, he was good-looking, charming, and brilliant too. Sharmila's parents hadn't objected to a love match, they were liberal-minded, progressive Indians and didn't insist on pushing her into an arranged marriage. Her father thought the world of Deepak, so the marriage had taken place quickly. But it was clear to Iris that there was something wrong. Neither of them was happy. Iris would have loved to have helped Sharmila, but had no idea how to.

'Would you like to play cards?' she asked brightly.

'Oh yes!' Sharmila smiled, and the smile reached her eyes for the first time that evening.

'Rummy?'

'Of course. What else?'

They played until after nine o'clock, by which time Iris was finding it hard to keep her eyes open, but she was glad to see that Sharmila had relaxed and was more like her old self. They had laughed and chatted their way through the evening, just as they had on many occasions when they'd first met.

'I'd best be going home,' said Iris, getting to her feet, yawning. 'I have to be back at the hospital early tomorrow morning.'

Immediately Sharmila's eyes clouded over and Iris knew she was worrying about Deepak again. It was late, so why hadn't he come home? But Iris didn't want to upset her by mentioning him.

'We must do this more often,' she said. 'Shall I come later in the week?'

'Oh yes. Yes please. I would love that.'

Cycling home in the cool night air, scented with jasmine and frangipani, Iris thought about how much she appreciated Sharmila's friendship and how much duller life in Nagabhari would be without her. They'd hit it off from the start, when they'd met at a reception for some visiting academics at the university. She'd only gone along at the last minute that evening to accompany her father. Her mother had flatly refused to go with him, pretending to have a fever, as she often did to get out of formal occasions she had no interest in. Iris had taken pity on Daddy and gone along in her mother's place.

Sharmila was amongst the Indian students who'd been hand-picked to attend. During one of the long and tedious speeches, Iris' eyes had strayed across the room and had caught Sharmila's gaze. She suspected that Sharmila was as bored as she was, so, after the speeches, when people were mingling, holding drinks and canapes, she made her way through the crowd and opened a conversation with her. That was three years ago, when she'd first got back from England and had almost given up trying to find a soulmate of her own age... but their first conversation almost ended in disaster.

'I saw you looking around the room during Professor Ramesh's speech,' Iris had said, by way of an opening gambit. 'Were you finding it a bit dull?'

'On the contrary,' Sharmila countered, her dark eyes twinkling. 'Professor Ramesh had a lot of interesting things to say. I was just looking round to gauge reactions. Most people seemed riveted.'

'Oh,' Iris was deflated, wondering how to respond. Sharmila couldn't have failed to notice how bored she had looked.

'I suppose,' Sharmila went on, 'Those who haven't studied John Donne might have found it hard to follow.'

'Of course,' Iris replied politely.

'I should just mention,' Sharmila went on, a teasing smile in her beautiful dark eyes, 'that Professor Ramesh is actually my father. And I helped him to write the speech.'

Then she burst out laughing. Such an infectious, bubbly laugh that Iris couldn't help joining in, even though she felt wrongfooted and foolish. They were friends from that moment on, spending time cycling in the countryside together, playing cards, discussing books, politics, their hopes for the future. After a year or so, Deepak came to Nagabhari and things changed subtly between them. They'd seen each other less after Sharmila's marriage but were no less close.

Needless to say, Iris' mother didn't approve, and the friendship had been the source of many bitter arguments.

'You should find someone from your own community to be friends with, instead of an Indian girl,' Delphine had said after she'd spotted Iris and Sharmila walking on the maiden together one day. 'It's really not appropriate.'

'Why not? What difference does it make? I've far more in common with Sharmila than any of the English girls in Nagabhari.'

'Well, what about Elspeth? Josie's always asking why you two don't spend more time together.'

'Elspeth and I don't have anything in common, Mummy. You know that. We're chalk and cheese.'

'Well, you could *try* at least. At least she's your own kind.'

'That's a beastly thing to say. How can you be so narrow-minded?'

'Now, now.' Her father stood in the doorway, wringing his hands.

'Oh, stay out of it, David,' Delphine snapped. 'It's none of your business.'

'It's very much my business,' he said stepping into the room. 'There's really no reason why Iris shouldn't be friends with Sharmila. She's a highly educated young woman and Professor Ramesh is a respected member of the academic community.'

'Poppycock and you know it,' Delphine countered, but she backed down and said no more on that occasion. Iris felt the weight of her disapproval constantly and tried to avoid mentioning Sharmila in her mother's presence.

Now, she drew up outside the Residence, her family home, and put her bike inside the veranda. As she opened the front door, her heart sunk when she heard raised voices coming from the living room. This wasn't unusual; her mother and father argued frequently. It always depressed her and mostly made her feel sad for her father.

'You're drunk, Delphine. You really should know when to stop.'

'Letting the side down, am I?'

'Well, it certainly doesn't do the side any good. And we need all the respect we can muster at the moment.'

'Hhmm, so I've heard.'

'What does that mean?'

Iris shut the door with a bang and they both stopped talking and turned to look at her. She saw embarrassment and guilt in both their faces.

'Hello, darling. Come and sit down,' said Delphine, patting the sofa beside her. 'We're just having a nightcap.'

'Your mother's having a nightcap, Iris. I've still got work to do. Where have you been?'

'Oh, just cycling around,' she said evasively, not wanting to add fuel to the fire by mentioning her visit to Sharmila. 'I needed some fresh air after the hospital. It was dreadful today. Overwhelmed with wounded soldiers from the front.'

'I know,' her father said. 'It's so worrying. Looks as though the Japs are finally trying to advance into India.'

'Some of the men were in a dreadful state.'

'Poor darling,' said Delphine. 'Sit down and have a brandy. It will do you good.'

'It's all right, Mummy. I think I'll just go to bed. I'm on the early shift at the hospital tomorrow.'

'Oh, Iris. Before you go,' said her father. 'I hope you don't have any plans for tomorrow evening. We've been invited to the palace for dinner. We'll have to be on the boat at six thirty. Are you free?'

'Oh, Daddy,' she breathed, sitting forward, her eyes shining, the traumas and exhaustion of the day temporarily forgotten. 'How marvellous. Of course I'll be able to make it.'

Later, as she drifted off to sleep under her mosquito net, her mind was restless. It flitted from the traumas of the ward with horrific visions of suppurating wounds and men groaning, twisting and turning in pain, to images of the majestic Lake Palace, its domes and archways lit up against an inky night sky. She couldn't wait for the next evening. The palace had occupied her dreams since childhood and at last she was going there again.

4

Dining at the palace with the royal family didn't sound quite such an enticing prospect when Iris' father told her more details. By that time, they were being driven by her father's syce along the bumpy road beside the lake towards the landing stage to take the maharajah's boat.

'Prince Ranjit is home for a few days apparently,' said her father. 'He's brought a couple of friends with him. Elspeth and some other youngsters from the club will be there too. The maharajah wanted Ranjit and his friends to have some young people as company.'

Iris' heart sank. Ranjit had been a spoiled, difficult child when they were young, constantly getting into trouble and playing pranks on his sisters and Iris. From what she'd heard on the grapevine, he hadn't changed. He'd become a playboy prince, getting into trouble in Oxford where he'd been sent by his father to study law. He was finally sent down from college without finishing his degree, for being repeatedly drunk and for driving his sports car onto the quad in front of the master's quarters. Since then, he'd become famous for his extravagant parties and expensive gambling habit. His friends were bound to be as boorish as Ranjit, Iris thought, and regretted having so readily agreed to go to the palace for dinner.

But it was impossible to get out of by then. They were almost at the ghat and in the dwindling light she could see the maharajah's elaborate boat drawn up against the jetty. How carefully she'd dressed for the evening, in her dark blue silk evening dress, her springy blonde hair tamed and twisted into a French pleat. She'd added glittering diamond earrings and necklace her father had brought her for her twenty first birthday, and high heels to complete the outfit. She glanced across at her mother. She was overdressed as usual, and heavily made up, but for once, she was sober. Iris couldn't help noticing that she looked a little anxious. Perhaps she wasn't looking forward to the evening any more than Iris herself was.

Despite her misgivings, she couldn't help feeling something of her old excitement return as they boarded the boat and were comfortably seated on velvet benches under a tasselled canopy. The boat was lit by lanterns, two on the bow, two on the stern, and manned by turbaned palace servants. She half expected them to get out oars and row the boat across to the palace, but as a concession to speed, a discreetly placed engine put-putted them across the lake.

Iris stared out across the rippling surface of the lake, that reflected the burning colours of the setting sun. She trailed her hand in the water, just as she used to as a child, and thought back over her day.

More soldiers had been admitted to the hospital, bringing the wards to breaking point. The surgeon, Dr Jefford, performed emergency operations round the clock: amputations, resetting bones, removing rotting flesh from wounds. Iris had to help prepare the men for surgery. As she removed their dressings and cleaned their wounds, her heart went out to those unfortunate young men again and again. The look in their eyes was always the same; a look of desperation and confusion. They'd come out to Burma to fight an enemy they had been told was unprepared for battle and inferior in every way. Each and every one of them had been shocked and terrified at the ferocity and skill of their opponent. It had been another day of harrowing sights and exhausting work, but something had happened during her lunch break that had given her food for thought.

She'd been sitting alone in the hospital refectory, grabbing some soup in between shifts, smoking a cigarette and reading a book as usual, when the tall, young doctor loomed over her. Her spirits sank. Conversation with him was always stilted and difficult.

'Do you mind if I sit here?' he asked shyly.

'Go ahead,' she gestured to the chair across the table. 'I have to be back on the ward in ten minutes though.'

He put his plate on the table and sat down opposite her.

'I'm Nigel Caldwell by the way. I know we've spoken briefly before, but we've never actually been introduced.'

He started to tuck into a mound of curry and rice.

Iris smiled. 'That's good to know. I'm Iris Walker. I'm actually just a volunteer here although everyone calls me "nurse".'

'Well, it's very good of you to give your time, Miss Walker. And from what I've seen, your skills are equal to those of the nurses.'

'I hardly think so. I've only had some basic training.'

She lapsed into silence. As on previous occasions she was finding it difficult to think of anything to say to this awkward young man, when to her surprise he said,

'I was wondering. Perhaps I could take you out one evening?'

She couldn't stop her face falling with shock. This was the last thing she expected and the last thing she'd wanted, too.

'Out?' She was uncomfortably aware that a faint blush was creeping into her cheeks. 'I'm not sure there is anywhere much to go in Nagabhari,' she blurted, trying to divert the conversation.

Nigel Caldwell was blushing deeply by now, his soft, grey eyes fixed on the table. 'Well, I know that. But I heard there are sometimes recitals at the university. Traditional Indian music.'

Traditional Indian music? She was well aware of the occasional recital of classical sitar music in the music faculty at the university, sometimes combined with poetry readings. She'd been along with Sharmila on a few occasions, but it was a shock to her that anyone else in the British community might find it remotely interesting, or even an acceptable way to spend an evening.

'Well, that sounds… interesting,' she said, keeping her voice neutral. 'But I'm quite busy at the moment. I often have to accompany my father to functions in the evenings.'

'Oh… yes. Your father is the British Resident here, isn't he?'

She nodded. 'Actually, this evening we're going to dine at the palace,' she said by way of explanation, but immediately regretted it. It sounded like boasting and also like a put-down to him.

'I see,' he said slowly. 'Well, I wasn't thinking of this evening. Another time maybe?'

'Perhaps,' she said, not having the heart to turn him down flat, but the idea of spending an uncomfortable evening in his company made her shrink inside. At the same time, she didn't want to appear superior. She knew, from hearing the nurses gossip, that Doctor Caldwell didn't come from the usual background shared by most Indian Civil Service officers and people who served the Raj. He wasn't either public school or moneyed. He was a scholarship boy from a working-class family in a northern town; intelligent and hardworking. It was why he struggled to make friends at the club, or anywhere else in the community in fact. Iris didn't want him to think that she was like all the others and that it was his humble background that was putting her off. Rather it was his awkwardness and the fact that spending a lunchtime in his company felt like an ordeal, let alone an evening with all the connotations that would bring with it.

She'd left the table quickly after that, leaving the subject hanging in the air. It troubled her that he might think her stand-offish or snobbish. She didn't want him to bracket her alongside Elspeth and the club crowd.

She sighed now, trailing her hand in the water, hoping that he wouldn't follow up the invitation with something more specific, but it was a vain hope. She would have to deal with the embarrassment of having to turn him down at some point. It was a pity, she reflected. She would have relished some male company and there was no one else in Nagabhari she would have liked to ask her out. None of the civil servants who worked for her father and frequented the club, none of the officers at the Indian Army HQ, where Elspeth's father was the commanding officer and where Elspeth herself had a desk job.

They were drawing closer to the palace now and she felt butterflies of excitement in her stomach. The building was lit up with fairy lights and lanterns, their reflections shimmering in the water.

'It looks so beautiful,' she murmured.

'Hardly the thing for wartime, though,' muttered her father. 'I have told HH, but to no avail. He's taken no notice. It's often the way with my advice.'

'Surely we're not in danger of air-raids here?' asked Iris in alarm.

'One never can tell. The Japs are in those hills up there and they have aircraft, that's for sure. And they have their sights firmly set on invading India.'

'Oh, surely not, David,' her mother burst out. It was the first thing she'd said on the whole journey and her voice sounded uncharacteristically nervy.

'You never know. But apart from that it sends quite the wrong messages. There are people suffering in this state. There's been a famine. He's had rebellions at every turn.'

'Well, please don't be grumpy about it and spoil the evening,' Delphine replied tersely, drawing her pashmina shawl about her and shivering.

It was the first time Iris' parents had exchanged a word all evening. The atmosphere in the boat had been decidedly frosty. They had sat apart, each with their own thoughts, staring out across the dark lake. Iris was used to that, but hoped fervently they would be civilised at dinner and not snap at each other and embarrass everyone as they sometimes did.

The boat had reached the landing stage. One of the boatmen jumped out and secured the ropes, then held a hand out to Delphine to help her ashore. Iris followed, glad of the boatman's help in her high heels. As she walked behind her mother along the jetty towards the steps that led up to the palace, she recalled all the times as a child she'd scrambled out of the boat ahead of her father and run up the steps, bursting with excitement just to be here.

A liveried servant met them at the top of the steps and guided them in through the palace entrance, and on through the echoing marble halls lit with flickering lanterns, to a vaulted central chamber, where people were already assembled with drinks. The men were dressed in dinner jackets, the women, apart from the maharanee, in evening dresses. The room was both beautiful and extravagant, framed by pillared archways, furnished with silk armchairs, and lit by many chandeliers.

The maharajah stepped forward and shook her father's hand.

'David! How good of you to come.' The maharajah was a handsome, urbane man, with a self-assurance that comes from a lifetime of privilege, and there was a certain charisma in his dark eyes that was compelling. He cast his gaze towards Iris and her mother and bowed his head appreciatively.

'And you've brought your charming ladies along. How wonderful.' His Oxford education shone through in his accent.

Delphine stepped forward and curtsied low, bowing her head in deference, then it was Iris' turn. She'd never had to do this as a child, and it felt odd, but Delphine had made her practice in front of the mirror before they set off. As she rose, she spotted the maharanee detaching herself from a huddle of guests and moving towards them.

'How kind of you to have come,' the maharanee said graciously, inclining her head. Iris caught a warning look from Delphine and she automatically curtsied again.

'Oh, please. No need for that,' the maharanee laughed, waving Iris to get up. She was an impressive woman, as beautiful as the maharajah was handsome, with luxuriant black hair, high cheekbones, and dancing eyes. She was dressed in a dark green silk saree trimmed with gold brocade. In one hand she held a champagne glass and in the other a cigarette in a long tortoiseshell holder. Iris knew her to be a strong woman, always out in the villages, helping the poor, campaigning for girls' education. She also knew that the maharanee was the maharajah's third wife. The other two, older wives, never appeared in public. They were in strict purdah and lived behind closed doors in the zenana – a private section in the palace.

'Ranjit is here. He will be delighted to see you. You remember him, Iris dear, from when you were a little girl?' the maharanee's eyes glittered with amusement. 'He was a naughty little boy back then, for sure.'

Iris smiled and glanced across at the huddle of people gathered around the prince at the other end of the room. Ranjit was holding forth, gesticulating to his audience, no doubt relating an amusing anecdote. Everyone else was silent, listening to him, amusement bubbling in their eyes, and when he finished and paused, they all burst out laughing and gave him a round of applause. He was tall and good-looking like his father, but there was an arrogance in the way he carried himself that was unmistakeable even from where Iris stood.

A gong sounded for dinner and, led by the maharajah, who took Delphine on his arm, everyone paraded through double doors to the palatial dining room next door. This room was even more impressive than the reception hall, with arches and pillars holding up a domed ceiling, painted and embellished with gold leaf, and a huge banqueting table set with linen and silver.

Iris found herself seated next to a young man, one of Prince Ranjit's friends. She sighed. Would she have to spend the evening listening to anecdotes about drunken exploits, fast cars and gambling? She couldn't wait for the meal to be over.

'We haven't been introduced,' he leaned towards her and held out his hand. 'Edward Stark.'

She took it and told him her name.

'Ah. You must be the Resident's daughter. I've heard a lot about you.'

'Really?' she was taken aback.

'Oh yes. Dr Jefford, the surgeon from the city hospital is here. There he is – at the other end of the table. He was just saying what a fabulous job you're doing on the ward.'

'Oh,' she hadn't noticed the surgeon amongst the crowd gathered around the prince, but glancing across the table she saw him now near the end, seated beside his wife, a stout, frumpy woman. He smiled gallantly and raised his glass to her.

'Well, it's very nice to be appreciated,' she said, taking a sip of champagne and thanking the bearer who placed a plate of dressed crab in front of her.

'I suppose a girl in your position doesn't *have* to help out,' he said. 'It's very good of you to do that.'

'I wouldn't have it any other way. I need to do something. And it's not much, really, in the great scheme of things.'

'Well, I'm sure it can't be easy. I've heard some of the injuries sustained in the field by our troops are hideous. And the jungle diseases they pick up too…'

'Yes! It's quite dreadful what has happened to some of them. Many are suffering from malaria, dysentery, beriberi.'

Edward Stark shook his head, concern and compassion in his eyes.

'Jungle warfare takes a terrible toll,' he said. 'Especially on those who aren't properly trained for it.'

She looked at him properly for the first time. The conversation wasn't taking quite the turn she'd expected. This man seemed serious, genuine, well-informed, with a keen interest in the fate of ordinary soldiers. It surprised her, as it chimed so well with her own feelings, and it was so different from what she'd been expecting. He was smiling at her. He had gentle brown eyes and wavy dark-blond hair. He was slightly built, but compact and lean-looking. Not skinny and angular like Nigel Caldwell. And contrary to expectations, he was quietly spoken, thoughtful and respectful.

'And how do you know Prince Ranjit?' she couldn't help asking. Even on five minutes acquaintance, she could tell that they were the most unlikely companions.

'Oh, Oxford. A few years back now. We were at the same college. We weren't in the same crowd there of course. Ran is far too glamourous and fast for the likes of me.'

'So, why are you here with him now?'

'Ah. Well, that's complicated,' he replied, rubbing his chin. 'I'm in the Indian Civil Service and a few of us are planning a mission into the Naga Hills.'

'Mission? Surely the hills are a bit dangerous at the moment?'

'Oh... it's nowhere near the fighting. No, it's to set up schools for the Naga tribes. Educate them, teach them English. Bring them into the 20th century by trying to persuade them to stop headhunting for good. It still goes on in remote parts you know, even though it was banned last century.'

'Well, that sounds dangerous enough in itself,' she teased and he laughed. She wondered briefly why he wasn't in the military, but she knew that some of the jobs in the ICS were reserved occupations.

'Not dangerous at all,' he said, his steady brown eyes on her face. 'Ranjit offered to fund the mission and to help us out with equipment and transport. It's in the interests of Ranipur state to keep the Nagas onside.'

'So, when are you going?' she asked.

'I'll be here for a few days. One of my colleagues is already here with us. Ronny over there,' he nodded across the table.

'An expert in the tribal languages of the Naga Hills. We're waiting for another chap. He knows the lie of the land and I don't think we'd be able to get up into the villages without him.'

Iris looked across the table at the other stranger in the group, who was sitting beside the prince. That must be Ronny, the colleague Edward was referring to. Iris felt a surge of relief that she was sitting next to Edward and not the other man. That man was older, with a Victorian-style beard. He wore gold-rimmed glasses and had an intellectual air about him. He was dressed somewhat eccentrically in a flowing white shirt, and was tucking into his meal seemingly unaware of the people around him.

'So, have you been in India long?' she asked, turning back to Edward.

'Oh yes. I came here before the war in '39. Drove out here from Blighty as a matter of fact with a few friends. In an old Morris.'

'You *drove*?' she laughed, incredulous. 'I've never heard of *anyone* doing that before. Why on earth would you do that?'

He scratched his head, smiling ruefully. 'Well, it's all got rather lost in the mists of time. I think it started out as a sort of wager in a pub and developed from there. Crazy really, when you think about it...' he trailed off, his eyes faraway, remembering.

'Tell me about it,' she asked, hardly aware that they had finished their starters and were on the next course. She took a forkful of food; it was top quality salmon, but she barely tasted it.

'Well, it was tricky sometimes,' he replied, 'On borders, and in various lawless countries we had to cross. In some places the roads weren't good either...'

'Go on?'

And so he told her. A tale of mishaps and adventures, of dodging or persuading authorities, of getting stuck on mountain passes, running out of fuel on remote roads. Having to find a way through where there were no proper roads at all.

When he'd finished, she shook her head in wonder, speechless. She'd never heard anything so exciting in all her life. It made her feel sheltered and parochial, and very unadventurous.

They were onto the sweets by now. Lemon souffle, with dessert wine to wash it down. Iris was vaguely conscious that she had barely said a word to the man on her other side. It was one of the staff officers stationed in Nagabhari, part of the club set. She had no desire to speak to him, and she sensed with relief that he was engaged in conversation with Elspeth who was seated on his other side.

'And what have you been doing since '39?' she asked Edward.

'Oh, a succession of quite menial, pen-pushing jobs in the ICS. Working for district officers in various stations around British India. The last one wasn't far from here, actually. In the next state along. I got involved in some protests over rice tax there and was held hostage by a group of angry village women until the D.O. announced a change in policy.'

'How extraordinary!' she exclaimed. 'Adventure seems to follow you around.'

'It was hardly an adventure,' he smiled. 'It was actually rather uncomfortable and a tad inconvenient too.'

She smiled into his eyes and he smiled back at her, and she sensed a connection between them. It sent chills all the way down her spine. She was overwhelmed with a powerful desire to get to know this man, to listen to his gentle, amusing voice for ever, to hear more about his adventures. In fact to find out all about him.

People were getting up from the table now. Some moving into the reception room for brandy, others going out onto the parapets to smoke.

'I need a cigarette,' Edward said. 'And a breath of air. Would you like a stroll outside? It's beautiful at this time of night.'

'I'd love that,' she said. They left the table and she followed him out through the reception hall, through the double doors and into the courtyard.

'Come this way,' he said, taking her arm, escorting her through a walled garden and out onto a hexagonal marble platform that was built out above the water. The arched openings looked out over the lake in every direction.

'This is magical,' she whispered, leaning out of one of the openings and taking a deep breath of the warm evening air. It was fresh out here on the lake and scented with the sweet smell of frangipani.

Edward lit a cigarette and handed her one. She took it and held it up to his to light.

It was a clear night and the inky sky was awash with tiny stars, their twinkling reflections dancing on the water. The only sound was the lake lapping at the palace walls below and, as she watched, high above them, a shooting star seared across the sky.

'This is a beautiful part of the world,' Edward said, leaning on the stone sill next to her. She could feel the heat of his body next to hers.

'It is,' she replied. 'I love it. I grew up here really, apart from the time I was in England.'

'So, you know all the interesting places around and about?'

She paused. 'Well, the places I know aren't necessarily what most people would find interesting.'

'Such as?'

'There are some ruined temples in the forest not too far from the town, and some caves and an abandoned palace in the hills in the other direction.'

'They sound fascinating to me,' he said.

There was the sound of footsteps in the walled garden and Iris' father appeared in the archway.

'So sorry to disturb you, darling,' he said mildly, 'but it's time for us to make a move.'

Then he cleared his throat and made his departure back into the walled garden, but his appearance had interrupted the flow of their conversation.

'Well, goodbye,' Iris said awkwardly, feeling the pulse in her throat and the panic rising. How could she leave like this, when they'd only just begun to get to know each other? She already felt bereft of his company, the great black void of boredom threatening to swallow her up again.

'Goodbye. It was wonderful to meet you,' he held out his hand, took hers and kissed it tenderly, sending thrills running through her.

She wished she could stay, but was acutely aware of her father hovering out there in the garden, of Mummy back inside the palace getting impatient. She left him standing there in the little tower. She could feel his eyes on her as she walked across the tiles of the walled garden to join her father, and it was like walking on air.

5

The next morning, a note arrived with the newspaper at breakfast time. Iris glanced out of the window. One of the palace servants waited on the veranda. She recognised his blue and red silk livery. It must be an urgent message to her father from the maharajah. Her father scanned the envelope briefly and passed it straight to her.

'It's for you, Iris darling.'

She took it, surprised. She didn't recognise the writing on the envelope and she hardly dared to hope that it had come from Edward Stark. She ripped it open and pulled out the note inside and her heart turned a somersault.

My dearest Iris,

It was wonderful to meet you last night. I have thought of nothing else but you since we said goodbye. Would you come out with me for a drive today? Our travelling companion has been delayed so I'm here for a few more days. If you would like to, please let me know when and where to pick you up. The servant will wait for a reply.

Yours, Edward

She wrote back, scribbling the note hastily while the

servant waited impassively on the porch. Her father watched her silently, munching his way through his morning kedgeree. He was far too discreet to ask her who it was from.

All day at the hospital, her mind returned again and again to Edward and a little thrill went right through her each time she remembered that he was collecting her after work. She went over their conversation many times, her heart beating quickly as she remembered some of the things she'd said that sounded naïve or crass as she played them back to herself. If only she was better educated, more sophisticated. How cossetted and parochial her conversation must have sounded to him.

The influx of wounded soldiers onto the ward had eased a little and some of the men who'd come in on the first day were now well enough to be discharged. As each one left, they thanked her, many of them adding a little joke; 'Til next time, nurse.' 'There'll be lots more battles, so you won't run out of customers!'

In amongst the goodbyes was the usual round of chores; dressing wounds, doling out food, ensuring each man took his medicine, emptying bed pans. The routine sometimes got her down, but today she was feeling more buoyant, and the sights and sounds of the ward, though still distressing, no longer had the power to horrify her. At lunchtime she carefully avoided Nigel Caldwell, making sure she went to the canteen early, while he was still on his ward rounds. She didn't want to have to suffer the embarrassment of being asked out by him again. Not that day.

In the afternoon, the time dragged terribly, and Iris found herself repeatedly checking the big white clock on the wall of the ward. At last, her shift came to an end and she dashed to the cloakroom, showered quickly and changed into her cornflower blue dress with little white flowers and a white collar that set off the blue of her eyes.

Edward Stark was driving one of the palace cars when he pulled up outside the front entrance of the hospital at five thirty. It was an open topped sports car, and Iris' heart leapt for joy when she saw him in the driver's seat.

'Hop in,' he said. He was dressed in an open-necked white shirt, his hair tousled and his skin flushed from the wind.

She got in quickly, not wanting any of the nurses to see her and start asking questions.

'Thank you for agreeing to come out with me,' he said, pulling out of the hospital forecourt. 'Where shall we go? You said you knew all the interesting places.'

It didn't much matter to Iris where they went, just being with him was enough.

'How about the caves I told you about?' she suggested. 'There are some ancient paintings in them. Would you like to see them? They are a few miles out of town, and the light will be fading by the time we get there…'

'There's a torch in the glove compartment. The darkness will just add to the excitement, won't it?' He flashed a smile at her as he accelerated down Hospital Road. Iris felt the wind in her hair and simultaneously the cares of the day melting away.

'Which way?' he asked.

'Left at the next junction and over the railway track. Then head for the hills.'

'Head for the hills! I like that,' he laughed. His laugh was infectious and she couldn't help joining in.

Soon they left the straggling huts and low buildings of the outskirts of town behind and were out on the open road heading towards the foothills of the Nagas. The engine was noisy and the wind rushing in their faces made conversation difficult, but Iris didn't want to pass the journey in silence.

'Tell me more about your mission to the Naga villages,' she asked, trying to pull back her hair that was whipping about her face.

'Oh, there's not much to tell really,' Edward shouted in response, 'Other than what I said yesterday evening. It's just government business. Nothing interesting, I can assure you.'

She wondered why he was being reticent about it now, but decided not to ask him anymore, rather to just enjoy the moment. The fact that she was here, actually sitting beside him in the maharajah's car, heading off for an evening's adventure, felt almost unreal. It was the sort of thing her soul had craved for the past three years. It was as if she was waking up after a long, deep sleep.

The sky was darkening as they got closer to the looming mountains and the sun was setting in the west behind them, casting a warm red glow over everything. Edward turned to smile at her and his face was illuminated by the setting sun, his hair streaked golden and red, his eyes a warm brown.

'It's not far now,' she said, smiling back.

'It doesn't matter. I could drive like this for ever.'

The road began rising as they reached the foothills to the Nagas and the engine on the old car strained to maintain the pace. After a few miles of struggling uphill and labouring around hairpin bends, they reached the beginning of the trail into the hills. They left the car on the verge and trekked up the steep path to the cave entrance. By this time the light was fading fast. Edward switched on the torch and lit up the way. A million insects danced in the beam of white light.

'It's here,' Iris said as they reached the cavernous opening that led through to a chain of limestone caves. A couple of bats flew out, darting above their heads. Edward took her arm.

'Come on then. Let's go in and see those paintings.'

They stepped into the hot, dank interior of the caves and Iris clutched his arm. If she'd been with anyone else she would have been afraid, but Edward was so steady, so fearless, that his strength gave her courage. They moved on and within a few paces there was no light from the entrance at all and the flickering torch their only light. Iris wondered briefly what would happen if the torch failed.

They came to the first painting – a beautiful, dreamlike image of horned buffalo, flying amongst exotic birds, decorated with fruit and flowers.

'Hey, that's marvellous,' Edward said. 'Incredible. How old are these paintings?'

'Seventh century, I think,' she said. 'But it's difficult to find anything much out about them. There are a few books in the university library.'

'I'm impressed,' he said, and she could tell from his tone that he was genuine. They moved on, through the chambers of the cave, further into the depths of the mountain, marvelling at the incredible paintings in each cavern, some of gods, others of battles, of warriors with spears, some on horseback charging at each other. Edward flashed his torch around, giving the scenes an added dimension. The colours were fabulous; terracotta, ochre, bright blues. As fresh as if they'd been painted the day before.

In the last cave, they came to some paintings of gods twisted in erotic poses, of phallic symbols, of women with swollen breasts, of figures entwined in impossible positions. Iris had never before ventured so far into the chambers, the darkness and dampness having always repelled her and she shrunk in embarrassment as she looked around at the paintings.

'I'm so sorry...' she faltered. 'I didn't know about these ones.'

'They're fabulous,' Edward replied, his voice steady, as if he was completely unfazed by what he was seeing. He didn't change his tone or shift about uncomfortably, but now she was even more aware of her bare arm tucked inside his, the feel of his body through his cotton shirt, their heat mingling.

'I read somewhere that there has always been a strong connection between the sensual and the divine in Indian art,' he said. 'They celebrate the body rather than hiding it as something sinful. Completely the opposite of our buttoned-up attitude.'

'Yes – I read something similar...' she said, feeling her embarrassment melt away.

'Well, shall we go?' he asked. 'We seem to have reached the end of the caves now.'

Back outside, he opened the car door and helped her back into the passenger seat and they set off back to Nagabhari. They drove in silence, blanketed in darkness, but it didn't feel awkward at all. It was the sort of silence that exists between two friends who have known each other a long time and are comfortable in each other's company.

When they drew up outside Iris' house, she thought about asking him in, but didn't want to subject him to her mother's scrutiny, or indeed to her shameless flirting. She wanted to keep him all to herself.

'Thank you for showing the caves to me,' he said, switching off the engine, his eyes on her face. 'They were amazing.'

'It was my pleasure,' she replied, thinking how inadequate those words sounded. At the same time her heart was beating anxiously. What if this was it, what if she never saw him again?

'Same time tomorrow?' he asked, as if reading her thoughts.

'Oh, that would be wonderful!'

That night, lying under her mosquito net, although exhausted, Iris struggled to sleep. Her mind was filled with images of Edward. Of his gentle smile, his easy humour, of the feel of the hard muscles in his arm next to hers. Their conversations played over and over in her mind, as did the words he'd written in his note; *I've thought of nothing else but you since we said goodbye...*

The next day, when he picked her up at the hospital after her shift, she suggested they should go to the bazaar.

'It's incredible. If you want the true flavour of Nagabhari you'll find it there,' she said. 'You won't find many British people in there, I'm afraid, though.'

'What a hardship,' he joked.

They parked up on the edge of the Old Town and walked side by side through the darkening backstreets, where women in brightly coloured sarees squatted on the pavement cooking over open fires and the smell of spices filled the air, towards the market hall. It was busy at that time of day, packed with people bargaining for fruit and vegetables, meat, shoes, pots and pans, silks, jewellery. Almost anything you could think of was on sale there and the aisles were thronging with noisy shoppers gossiping and bargaining at the tops of their voices. Iris had been to the market hall before but she'd never had the courage to purchase anything. They wandered the length of the central aisle, gazing at the colourful produce. Towards the far end of the building, there was a section of the market given over to jewellery. Edward made straight for one of the stalls and started examining the beautiful pieces on sale.

'By the way, what's your birthstone?' he asked suddenly, turning to Iris.

'Birthstone?'

He nodded. 'Everyone has a birthstone. Which month were you born in?'

'January.'

'Well then, your birthstone would be garnet.'

He leaned forward and spoke to the stallholder. Iris was impressed to hear that his Hindi was fluent. The man started producing trays of garnet jewellery; rings, pendants, bracelets, necklaces from behind the stall. Iris looked at the sparkling, burgundy-coloured stones. How beautiful they were.

'Do you like this pendant?' Edward asked, picking out a teardrop-shaped jewel set in silver on a delicate silver chain.

'It's beautiful,' she said, 'but...'

'No buts. I'd like to buy it for you.'

'Oh Edward, it's far too expensive!'

'You've underestimated my bargaining skills,' he laughed and turned back to the stallholder and began to haggle with him.

Iris watched, half-amused, half embarrassed that he was intent on buying her this expensive gift. They hardly knew each other, after all. She began to look around, wondering what she could give him in return.

Finally, the bargain was clinched, Edward handed over some notes and the stallholder began wrapping up the jewel in tissue paper.

'You shouldn't have done that,' she said. 'It's too kind.'

'Whyever not? I saw the jewellers there and thought I'd like to buy you something to remember me by.'

'Oh,' she said, dropping her eyes, remembering that he was leaving soon. In a matter of days in fact. They might never see each other again. 'Well, it's incredibly generous of you. I'll treasure it. But I don't like to think of you leaving.'

He took her chin in his hand and, turning her face towards

his, looked deep into her eyes. 'I'll be leaving, but I'll come back to see you after the mission. And we can write. Being with you has been incredible. It's made me feel alive for the first time in an age.'

His eyes were locked on hers and she could feel the strength of his emotion just from his look. The clamour and heat of the market faded into the background, and it was as if nothing else in the world mattered and the two of them were completely alone, totally absorbed in each other. She knew exactly how he felt.

'Me too,' she whispered.

Then someone bumped into Edward from behind and he stumbled, grabbing onto her arms. It jolted them back into the present moment.

'I guess we'd better carry on now,' he said. 'We're getting in the way.'

'Oh, but I haven't bought you a present yet!'

'There's absolutely no need for that,' he said, taking her hand and starting to push on through the crowd.

They carried on through the market, pausing to wonder at giant fruit, to drink cane sugar from a stall and eat spicy pakoras at another one. The time flew past and by the time they were thinking about leaving, some stallholders were packing up for the evening.

They wandered back to the car through the dark streets hand in hand, the scent of evening fires hanging on the air. Back at the car, he leant in and kissed her for the first time and she slid her arms around his neck and pulled him close. She wanted to hold on to that moment for ever. She never wanted to let him go.

6

Nagabhari, India, 1985

Iris stood there, her palms on the stone sill of one of the openings in the little tower, leaning out over the rippling waters of the lake, thinking back over those few magical days in 1944. Every hour, every minute of the time she and Edward had spent together, were seared into her memory. She treasured those memories as if they were precious jewels. But she'd kept them buried for over forty years, almost afraid to take them out and examine them. It was only now that she was back here, in the very place they'd first met, that she let those memories return to her. And once they'd been released, they were flooding back.

She fingered the garnet pendant he'd given her at the bazaar that night absently. She'd kept it hidden away, like her memories, throughout her marriage to Andrew. It was only after his death, when she was clearing out the cupboards, that she'd come across it. It seemed appropriate to wear it on her trip back to India. Standing here, in the place where everything had started, that balmy evening in '44, the memories became so vivid that it felt as if it had all happened yesterday, not over forty years ago.

'Remembering the old days?' She jumped as Elspeth's hectoring voice broke into her thoughts. She turned round, letting go of the pendant.

'This is where you met lover boy, isn't it?' Elspeth said, walking towards her.

'Lover boy?'

'Yes – that friend of Ranjit's from his Oxford days. Edward somebody. You tried to keep it quiet, but we all knew about it.'

'Oh,' Iris was instantly deflated. It felt as if the memory were somehow sullied by Elspeth's comments. They must have all been gossiping about her at the club, when she'd been thinking how discreet she and Edward had been. Elspeth was looking triumphant now, seeing the dismay on her face.

'Well, I didn't know that,' she said quietly, looking away.

'Shall we take a look at the old place then?' asked Elspeth. She looked refreshed now. A few minutes rest in the fresh air had revived her.

They walked back through the walled garden and in through the arched entrance, and on through the marbled halls towards the inner sanctum of the palace. Now denuded of furniture, these once gracious rooms appeared shabby, a shadow of their former selves. Paint was peeling from pillars, there were bird droppings in corners. Painted signs had been stuck on the walls to guide the visitor; *Reception Hall, Drawing Room, Dining Hall*. They only added to the impression that the glory days were gone. The building seemed to be living off its past triumphs.

They reached a small museum in the huge central hall that had been the dining room in the maharajah's day. Where the great banqueting table had been, a few dusty glass cabinets had been installed. Beside them stood mannequins of the maharajah and maharanee wearing their most fabulous silk outfits, studded with gems and embroidered with gold thread.

'It doesn't really capture the spirit, does it,' said Elspeth, wandering around the glass cabinets that displayed jewellery, china and ornaments that had once belonged to the royal family. On the wall a few old photographs hung, grouped together. Iris wandered over to take a look at them, curious.

There were a few grainy photographs of the maharajah's cars, lined up in his garage block in the city. Her heart leapt as she recognised the open-topped Ford that Edward had ferried her around in back in 1944. Then there were several pictures of the royal family, some posing with rifles in front of tigers and stags they had shot, others of them standing in stiff groups, bedecked in jewellery, and in yet others they posed in western dress. There was one of Ranjit in a three-piece suit and high collar standing in front of an Oxford college. Iris smiled, recognising fondly these people from her youth. Wherever were they now?

Then there was one of a larger group, of British and Indian people standing together. It looked as though it had been taken after a formal reception or dinner. With a jolt she recognised her parents, standing either side of the maharajah, with the maharanee on the other side of her father. All were smiling, including Delphine. It surprised Iris how young and beautiful her mother looked. She was dressed in a shimmering white evening gown, diamonds at her throat, her blonde hair swept back from her face, her high cheekbones and full lips giving her a glamourous, film-star look. Iris had known her mother was beautiful, but Delphine had always seemed so grumpy that her face had rarely lit up in a smile. This was the first time Iris had seen a photograph of her smiling broadly, her even white teeth on display.

'Mummy actually looks happy here,' she remarked to

Elspeth. Elspeth stomped over, leaning on her stick. She bent forward and peered through her glasses at the photograph.

'Stands to reason,' she remarked. 'Oh, and there's my father and mother too. In the back row. All dressed up for the occasion.'

Iris frowned, wondering what Elspeth meant by her remark, but was afraid to provoke any further barbed comments by asking.

'Well, the old place *has* gone downhill, hasn't it?' Elspeth said looking around her at the grubby walls. 'Shall we make a move? It will be getting dark soon and we don't want to miss supper.'

'Yes let's. It's a bit disappointing really. So sad to see it like this. Shall I take your arm?'

They moved slowly out through the once grand rooms and onto the parapet above the landing stage. Going down the steps to the jetty, Elspeth clung to Iris' arm so hard that she was a little afraid they both might slip. It would be a disaster if Elspeth fell and sustained a further injury.

As they left the Lake Palace on the boat, Iris looked back sadly at the crumbling old building that held so many happy memories for her. She was sitting in the bow of the boat facing backwards and as they drew further and further away from the palace, it gradually began to look more like the palace of her dreams. She wanted it to stay that way.

'I'm glad I've seen it, but I wouldn't go back there,' she said, more to herself than anyone else.

'Me neither,' Elspeth said stoutly. 'Shame to see the old place like that. Better to remember it as it was.'

At supper, which consisted of copious quantities of lamb curry and rice, Elspeth attacked the food with gusto, shovelling it into her mouth as fast as she could.

'That lake air made me hungry. You know I have missed the old place down the years,' she confided.

'I thought you loved England,' Iris replied, surprised.

'Well, I have to admit, England does have its benefits. I mean, life in India is hard, isn't it? The heat, the poverty, the bureaucracy, the difficulty getting anything done... but no, I do have a soft spot for it.'

'Oh, me too!' said Iris warmly. 'England could never replace it for me. I always hankered after coming back.'

'I have to confess that life in England for me never really matched up to my childhood in India. It was more comfortable, of course, but... well, it just wasn't the same.'

'You do surprise me, Elspeth,' Iris said, genuinely touched that Elspeth had been prepared to confide this to her. It was the first time she'd opened up to Iris about anything.

'Oh well,' said Elspeth as they finished their meal. 'I think I'll turn in early. As I said, all that fresh air has quite done for me.'

After she'd seen Elspeth to her room, Iris went to her own room, but it was early and she wasn't ready to turn in quite yet. Instead, she smothered herself in insect repellent and went outside to sit on the veranda. The sky was clear that night and the stars were as bright as they had been the night she met Edward. She stared up at them, thinking about him, trying to picture his face, to recall the sound of his voice. It was hard after so many years, but suddenly she realised there might be a way to help her recapture the essence of him; her diary. She knew that she was ready. Now that she was here in Nagabhari and had been to visit the Lake Palace. She hurried inside and retrieved it from her bag, then, settling down under the lamp on the veranda, she opened the little book. There was the photograph of Edward, tucked between the pages, staring out of the leather frame.

She hadn't looked at it in years, but those eyes still drew her in, all these years later.

The diaries began in November 1943, a few days before she'd started helping out at the city hospital. She remembered deciding to write it. Initially, she'd intended just to record her thoughts after each shift, thinking it might help her decide whether she wanted to make nursing a career. Reading it back now, it started out with rather boring, repetitive accounts of her days on the wards, of the tasks she'd carried out, of her impressions of the doctors and nurses and the patients she was there to care for. Occasionally, those descriptions were interspersed with lively accounts of her evenings with Sharmila, or her anecdotes about members of the club. But the diary came fully alive on the day of the influx of wounded soldiers from the front. Reading it now brought back the memory of the noises and smells of the ward, the intense suffering of the men and the efforts and exhaustion of the staff. She turned the page to read about the evening she'd met Edward.

'He's everything I've ever dreamed of in a man; adventurous, kind, fascinating, interested in the world and living life to the full. A true kindred spirit,' she'd written when she'd got home that night. The girlish infatuation leapt off the page, reading it now. But she knew it was more than just that. She'd fallen deeply in love that night, and although that love had been in abeyance for many years, it had lasted for four decades. She read on until her eyes were drooping, then went inside to bed, with fresh images of those days filling her thoughts and dreams.

She slept heavily, and in the morning dragged herself out of bed and knocked on Elspeth's door.

'We'll be late for breakfast,' she said in response to a groan from the other side.

'Don't want any breakfast,' Elspeth moaned. Alarmed, Iris turned the handle and went inside. The room smelled stale and Elspeth was slumped in bed, her face sweaty and pale.

'Got a dreadful upset stomach,' she said. 'I've been up and down all night. That beastly curry. I knew I would suffer afterwards.'

'Oh Elspeth, I'm so sorry. How awful for you. Is there anything I can get you?'

'Could you get me some soda water?'

'I'll try.'

The hotel manager was full of concern when Iris told him of Elspeth's illness and sent one of the waiters along to her room with some flowers and a bottle of soda water. Iris sat down alone in the restaurant, secretly relieved to be alone for once and to have the prospect of a day without Elspeth's constant carping.

As the waiter brought her porridge and coffee, she opened her India guide book, scanning the pages on Nagabhari for places to visit. She toyed with the idea of hiring a taxi and going out to the caves in the hills, but then realised there was probably a lot to see in the town itself first. There was a pull-out map of the area. As she unfolded it, her eyes alighted on the university, and the wide, spacious avenues of the campus on the east side of the town towards the lake. She thought of Sharmila and everything that had happened in the days before Iris had left India for good. Again, suppressing the guilt she always felt at having let their correspondence lapse, she wondered if Sharmila could still be living in that little bungalow along University Road all these years later. And then she realised that that was where she must go today. It was an ideal opportunity while Elspeth was laid up in bed. She would go and look up her old friend Sharmila.

7

Nagabhari, India, January 1944

Working through her routine chores at the hospital during those dreamy days in the early part of '44, Iris was aware that Edward's visit was likely to come to an end one day soon. But whenever that unwelcome thought arose, she pushed it aside, not wanting to contemplate that yawning chasm of emptiness that was bound to engulf her once he left.

The situation was brought home to her when one day, she was wandering back to the ward down the hospital corridor carrying a pile of freshly laundered sheets. She looked up to see Nigel Caldwell walking in her direction. Her heart sank, she had no desire to speak to him, but there was no avoiding him.

'Good morning Iris,' he said.

'Good morning,' she said, not knowing whether to address him as 'Doctor' or 'Nigel'.

'I'm glad I've bumped into you. I've been meaning to talk to you.'

'Oh?' her heart speeded up. She knew what was coming.

'Yes. There's one of those concerts at the university next week. Thursday evening. I was wondering if you'd like to go?'

'I can't I'm afraid,' she said, colour creeping into her cheeks at the awkwardness of the situation. 'Father has asked me to keep that evening free for an official engagement.'

She tried to keep her voice steady and her eyes on his. It was a lie, but a white one. Fleetingly, she wondered what she actually would be doing the following Thursday. Edward would surely have departed for the hills by then and she would be alone and at a loose end. Even so, she would rather spend the evening on her own, treasuring her memories, than go anywhere with Nigel.

'Oh?' he asked, raising an eyebrow, and it was clear from his tone that he didn't believe her. 'I understand. Another time perhaps?'

'Perhaps,' she said, dropping her eyes to the floor. It was far too embarrassing to come clean and tell him that it was highly unlikely that she would ever agree to go out with him, but as she hurried back to the ward she pondered the unpalatable thought that soon Edward would be gone and her choices of companions and entertainment would be as limited as they'd been before he'd arrived.

That evening, Edward collected her in the maharajah's car as usual. As she hopped in, he kissed her tenderly and said, 'Where to tonight?'

She noticed a difference in his tone. He sounded subdued, and a little anxious.

'There's a deserted temple in an abandoned village a few miles out of town. Would you like to see it?'

'That sounds interesting. Yes, let's go.'

Iris smiled to herself, patting the pocket of her dress. At lunchtime, she'd slipped out to the bazaar and bought Edward a pair of silver cufflinks. She'd asked the stallholder to engrave intertwined initials E&I on them, and she couldn't wait to give them to him and see his face as he opened the little box.

He didn't speak much during the drive and when Iris glanced at him, she experienced a prickle of worry at his silence.

'Are you alright?' she asked anxiously, and he rewarded her with one of his dazzling smiles.

'Of course. And all the better for seeing you.'

She guided him off the main road and down a maze of unmade tracks, dust belting from the tyres, through a collection of huts where chickens and pigs rooted about and the villagers came out to stare out the motor car passing through. They drove on, into a forest of bamboo and eucalyptus trees, until the ruins of the temple, nestled in the undergrowth, appeared in front of them.

'It's here!'

Edward parked the car and they clambered out.

'Shall we go and explore?' she said, taking his hand.

'Yes, but first, let me kiss you,' he said, leaning against the car door and pulling her close to him. She melted into his embrace, feeling his heart beat against hers as he kissed her.

'I've got something to tell you,' he said as he let her go.

'Oh?'

'My other colleague is due to arrive at the Lake Palace this evening. And that means we will be leaving for the hills at first light tomorrow.'

She didn't reply. She couldn't. She had to let the body blow sink in. Even though she'd known this was coming, it was still a shock and she found herself fighting back the tears.

'I'll miss you terribly,' she said, lifting her eyes to his.

'I'll miss you too, but I'll come back for you, like I said. And we can write.'

'Do you think they have post up in those villages?'

'Some of the bigger ones do. I'll give you an address. We might not be staying in that particular village, but we should be able to collect letters from there. I'll write whenever I can.'

'How long is your mission?'

'Not precisely sure at the moment. A few weeks. A couple of months perhaps.'

He took her hand and they made their way between the towering teak trees towards the temple ruins.

'Who is he?' she asked as they walked. 'Your other colleague. What does he do?'

'Well, he's actually an engineer by trade. Although he speaks the Naga language too. He's spent time in the hills before.'

'Why do you need an engineer?' she asked, curious.

'Ah – well, since we're up there, we were hoping to help them with their water supplies. Kill two birds, as it were.'

'And you're *sure* you're not going anywhere near the fighting?'

He laughed and squeezed her hand. 'It's very sweet of you to be concerned, but no, we're not going anywhere near the front.'

They had reached the remains of the old temple now. The tumbledown walls and dilapidated steps were half-submerged in jungle growth. Scattered amongst them were broken sculptures; faces, arms and legs of stone gods, broken and left to be taken over by the voracious undergrowth.

'This is extraordinary,' said Edward, looking around at the scattered ruins. 'Do you know why the temple was abandoned?'

'There's a local myth that it was cursed by Shiva a couple of hundred years ago. After that, no one wanted to worship here anymore.'

'University library again?'

She smiled and nodded and they strolled, hand in hand around the ruins. There was no need for words. There was so much unsaid between them, but it didn't seem to matter. They would meet again and when they did there would be plenty of time to talk.

'Oh. I nearly forgot. I've got something for you,' she said, pulling out the little box and handing it to him. He opened it, his eyes widening as he examined the cufflinks.

'They're beautiful! You shouldn't have done that though.'

'Whyever not? I'm hoping that when you wear them you'll think of me.'

'I will think of you anyway,' he said, bending forward and kissing her again.

'Shall I come and say goodbye in the morning?' she asked when they emerged from the kiss.

'Best not. We're starting out incredibly early and I'm no good at goodbyes. Better to say it when I drop you off at home. When there's just the two of us.'

As they came out of the woods and walked towards the car the sky was darkening. Iris felt a wave of panic that the evening was almost over. They would get in the car and he would drive her home for the last time. This delicious interlude in her life would be over. How would she bear it?

On the drive home, Edward held her hand whenever he wasn't changing gear and kept glancing over at her and smiling, but they didn't talk much. When they finally drew up outside her house he said,

'I haven't got a picture of you! I'd love to have one to take with me. Do you have one you could give me?'

'Alright. Wait here. I'll see what I can find.'

She raced inside the house and to her bedroom. There was a small black and white picture on her dressing table taken when she came back to India from London. It was a couple of years old, but it was flattering and she'd always been proud of it. When she came out of her room, Delphine was peering out of the window.

'Who's that out there in the maharajah's car, darling?'

'Oh, just someone I know.'

'It's that chappie from the palace, isn't it? Ranjit's friend? You should ask him in. Not have him waiting out there like a servant.'

'It's fine, Mummy. He's going now anyway.'

But as she reached the car she knew Delphine would still be watching from the window. How could she say goodbye like that, exposed to her mother's scrutiny?

'Can you drive me to the end of the road?' she asked, getting back in beside him.

He laughed. 'Whatever you want.'

'My mother's looking out of the window...'

'Enough said,' he laughed again, starting up the engine and accelerating out of the drive. He parked a few houses along from the Residence and took her into his arms and kissed her again. Although she didn't want the kiss to end, she knew it must. She was already mourning the loss of these precious moments. At last she broke away and said, 'You'd better go.'

'Would you like this?' he asked, fishing in his jacket pocket and handing her a small photograph, in a leather frame. In it he looked older, more serious somehow.

'Oh, and here's the address in the village,' he said, handing her a piece of paper. He must have written it before coming out. 'I know yours already. I'll write as soon as I am anywhere near a post office.'

'Goodbye then,' she said, kissing him one last time, then climbing down onto the road. He blew her another kiss, started up the engine and she stood watching as he drove away into the darkness.

Blinded by tears, she ran back to the Residence and up the front steps. Delphine was standing in the doorway.

'Are you alright, darling?' her face full of concern, she opened her arms. 'Come for a hug.'

Iris let herself be folded into her mother's arms and sobbed on her shoulder, just as she used to as a little girl when she'd hurt herself.

'I know you think I don't understand, darling,' said Delphine. 'But I do. I really do.'

8

The days that followed Edward's departure felt like pure torture. Iris went through them like a sleep-walker, barely noticing what she was doing, what people said to her. She hardly touched her food either, she simply had no appetite. But going to the hospital each day turned out to be a lifeline during those dark days. It gave her something to get out of bed for in the mornings, something to focus on other than her own misery.

On the third day after Edward had left for the hills there was another influx of soldiers from the front line. They had been brought down from the mountains where the fighting with the Japanese was getting fierce again. Once again, the staff on the ward were under huge pressure. But this time they were prepared for the shocking injuries sustained by some of the troops. It no longer sickened Iris to have to bathe a splintered leg or clean out a suppurating stomach wound. Once again though, she was disturbed by that look in all the soldiers' eyes; dazed shock and bewilderment at what they'd been through. Her heart went out to them in their distress and she redoubled her efforts to do whatever she could to make them comfortable.

That evening she went to see Sharmila.

'You look different,' Sharmila said instantly as the bearer showed Iris in. 'I've been expecting you to visit for days.'

'Oh!' Iris was instantly full of remorse. 'I'm so sorry, Sharmila. I should have been in touch. How could I have forgotten my promise?'

'It's alright,' Sharmila said. 'I realised you must have been busy. You look full of mystery, though. What *has* happened to you? Come and sit down and tell me all about it.'

So, Iris followed Sharmila through to her sitting room and, while sipping jasmine tea and nibbling pakoras and samosas, she told her all about meeting Edward, about where they'd been for the past few evenings, and about her feelings for him.

'I understand. I know just how you feel,' Sharmila said, clasping Iris' hands in hers, her eyes shining. 'I was just the same when I met Deepak. I couldn't eat, couldn't sleep, and yet I felt more alive than I'd ever felt before.'

But then a hint of sadness entered her eyes.

'And how is Deepak?' Iris asked gently. 'You were worried about him last time I came.'

Sharmila sighed heavily and shrugged. 'Things carry on much as before,' she said. 'He comes home late each evening. He drinks too much alcohol. I can't be sure he isn't involved with the Quit India campaign because he won't tell me where he's been. But... well in a way, I sometimes hope it *is* the Quit India campaign.'

'What do you mean?'

'Isn't it obvious? Sometimes I worry that there might be someone else.'

'Oh no, surely not, Sharmila,' Iris said, genuinely shocked, 'Deepak loves you. He's devoted to you.'

'I used to think that, yes. But I know there's a lot about his past that he won't tell me. He seems to have something to hide because he freezes up every time I ask about his life before Nagabhari. It frightens me that there's so much I don't know about him.'

'Oh, I'm sure there's nothing to worry about,' said Iris, putting her arm around Sharmila's shoulders. It distressed her to see her friend like this. It was such a contrast to how she'd been during the early days of her marriage.

'I wish I could do more to help you,' she said.

'You help more than you can know just by being my friend. It's good to know you're here for me,' said Sharmila.

Later, when she got home to the Residence, Delphine was sitting alone in the drawing room under the whirring fans. In front of her on the coffee table was a whisky glass and a half-empty decanter.

'Where have you been, Iris? I was worried about you.' Her mother's speech was slurred.

'Oh, just seeing a friend.'

Her mother gave her a knowing glance. 'Oh, I understand. *That* friend.'

But she didn't say any more about it, and Iris was glad to let the subject drop.

'Come and sit down with me, darling,' said her mother, patting the cushion beside her on the sofa.

'I'm tired, Mummy. I need to go to bed.'

'But I'm *worried* about you. You've not been yourself since that friend of Ranjit's left town. You haven't been to the club once, you're hardly eating.'

'I never went to the club anyway.' Iris relented and crossed the room to sit beside her mother.

'Well, you really should. There are lots of young people

there in the evenings and it might take you out of yourself. You look terribly miserable.'

'I can't help it,' Iris sighed. 'I miss him dreadfully. It's as simple as that.'

'I know exactly how you feel, darling,' her mother said, putting an arm around her and hugging her tight, but looking into her mother's bleary eyes Iris couldn't imagine that she could possibly understand. Surely, she'd never felt this fierce, burning, all-consuming passion for Daddy? It was impossible to contemplate.

The next evening, when Iris got home from the hospital, there was a letter for her propped up on the hall table. Her heart leapt as she recognised the handwriting. She snatched it up, ran up to her room and threw herself on the bed, ripping the envelope open.

My dearest Iris,

I was desperately sad after we said goodbye the other evening. Meeting you and spending time with you has made me happier than I can say, and now we're apart I'm missing you every second of the day. I can't wait until this mission is over and I can hold you in my arms again and cover your sweet face in kisses.

Life up here in the villages is very quiet and uneventful and, it has to be said, my travelling companions are worthy souls but they aren't great company in the evenings. The villagers are friendly and hospitable, but it's taking time to win them round. They aren't keen on outsiders coming in and telling them what to do, so we have to act with great sensitivity. Luckily both my companions are fluent in their language and I now know enough to get by.

We always dine with the villagers in their communal longhouse, then turn in early for bed. The others are asleep straight away, but I lie awake thinking of you, of your beautiful face, your sparkling blue eyes and your quick wit. I think constantly of my good fortune in meeting you and that we had those few wonderful evenings to get to know one another. I didn't have the courage to say this to your face, Iris darling, but I have fallen head over heels in love with you.

I'm not sure how reliable the postal service is in these hills, but if this does get to you, please write to me and tell me how you are, and let me know if my feelings are reciprocated. I will be waiting for your letter every second of every day.

Your ever loving,

Edward.

She read it over and over, her heart soaring. She was scarcely able to believe her good fortune. She went straight to her desk in the corner of the room and began to write a reply. It was difficult. She'd never written to anyone in those terms before. In fact, she'd never felt this way about anyone before. She made several false starts, screwing up her efforts and throwing them in the bin. In the end, she was vaguely satisfied with what she'd written.

My dearest Edward,

I can't tell you how happy I was to get your letter. I've been counting the seconds since we parted and missing you constantly. The evenings we spent together were the happiest of my life and I can't wait to see your dear face again and hold you in my arms. Of course I reciprocate your feelings! I love you. I think I loved you from the very first evening, when we were out on the balcony at the Lake Palace and you lit my cigarette and smiled at me. I just knew.

Life here goes on just as before. The hospital has been busy again with casualties from the front. Those poor boys. More and more of them are coming in every day. We do our best but for many of them it's a losing battle. I hope you are safe and that you are a long way from the fighting. I couldn't bear to think you were in danger.

Please write to me again as soon as you can. I am so miserable

without you and your letter has been the only thing that has bright-
ened my days since you left.

With all my love,

Iris

Then, exhausted with the effort of writing and feeling able
to relax for the first time since Edward had left, she fell into a
deep sleep.

In the morning, after breakfast, she asked the head bearer
to take her letter to the post office, and then she cycled off to
the hospital, her heart singing with joy. That joy carried her
through the next few days. Then she started wondering if her
letter had arrived and looked out for a reply each morning.
The days passed but no reply came. She began to wonder if
the bearer had actually posted her letter to Edward at all, and
kicked herself for not taking it to the post office herself. One
day she decided to question him about it.

'Viraj, you know I asked you to post a letter the other day?'

'Yes, Iris mem. I took it to the post office just as you asked.'

'So, you posted it then. Are you sure it went?'

He looked at her blankly. 'Of course, Iris mem. The lady
took it from me. I paid for the stamp.'

'How much did the stamp cost?'

'Two rupees, Iris mem. I took it from memsahib
Delphine's housekeeping.'

'And did they give you a receipt?'

He shook his head gravely. 'I didn't ask. I'm sorry, mem. I
not know you wanted receipt.'

'But you're absolutely *sure* you posted it.'

'Yes mem. Of course.'

He shuffled away, his face troubled. Iris felt a pang of guilt.
The servants hated any suggestion that they weren't trusted
and she knew he would be feeling hurt and insulted, but she
had to know.

The days crawled by and still no letter came. She waited in the front hall feverishly each morning for the post, but each day her hopes were dashed. Her mind went into overdrive. Had she said something in her letter to Edward that had put him off? She went over and over each and every word she'd written a thousand times, but couldn't think that anything she'd said could have upset him. Perhaps the letter had simply never arrived. It was a bit of a longshot after all, writing post restante to a post office in a far-flung village in the Naga Hills. The post in India was erratic at the best of times, but in those hill villages, and in wartime too, the chances of it arriving safely were surely quite slim.

After a week of letting her thoughts run wild about what had happened to the letter, she decided to write again. She sat down at the table in her bedroom and poured her heart out to Edward. She told him how worried she'd been not to have received a reply to her first letter and reiterated her love for him and the fact that she was missing him and waiting for him all the time. She finished with the words,

Please write back to me, Edward. A letter from you would mean everything to me and would set my mind at rest at least to some extent. You can't imagine how anxious not hearing from you has made me feel. I think about you night and day and live for the moment when I hear from you again. With all my love, Iris.

She sealed it up and addressed it to the post office in Nangtek, just as she had the previous one. Then she took it downstairs and put it on the hall table, but immediately snatched it up again. This time she wasn't going to leave anything to chance.

The next day, during her lunch break at the hospital, instead of going to the canteen, she got on her bicycle and pedalled through the old town to the central post office. Her heart sank when she saw that there was a long queue snaking out of the door. There was nothing for it but to wait. It took a good twenty minutes for her to reach the front and by that time she'd given up all hope of eating lunch that day. Not that it mattered, her stomach was so churned up with nerves that she had no real desire to eat.

The Indian lady behind the counter raised her eyebrows when she saw the address on the envelope.

'Post only goes up into that area one time a week and you've just missed it for this week. It goes on Tuesdays.'

Iris bit her lip. She was so wound up, her instinct was to cry but with a supreme effort of will she managed to hold the tears back.

'If it goes with the next delivery, when will it get there?'

'About ten days from now.'

'Alright.' She had no choice. She paid the money and watched the woman stamp the letter and throw it carelessly into a pile. She turned away knowing that she just had to trust that it would get there.

So the feverish wait began again. The ten days passed, then a few more days before she began looking out for the postman each morning. But nothing came and once again she began thinking the worst. She kept thinking about that pile of letters the woman in the post office had tossed it onto. Would it have been sorted properly? Would it have reached its destination? Would Edward have been back to Nangtek yet to collect it?

And if it hadn't arrived, if neither of her letters had arrived, what would Edward be thinking? Was he wondering if he'd said something in *his* letter that had put her off and stopped her writing, or would he have just put it down to the unreliable nature of the postal service? Then another worry entered her mind, to add to all the others. What if something had happened to him? He'd said they were going to be miles from the front, but maybe they'd strayed off course.

After a further week of torturing herself with these thoughts she wrote yet another letter. This one was much shorter and simply inquired whether he had got her previous letters and asked again for him to write to reassure her that he was alright. She made sure that she went on a Monday to post it so that it would go the next day. As she left the post office she promised herself that she wouldn't write again. That if there was no response this time, she would try to put it all behind her.

So once again she began the long wait for a response. And again it was to no avail. Day after day she looked out for the post, but no letter came from Edward. The worry of not knowing and the impotence of not being able to do anything to find out made her very low. She could barely concentrate on anything and a couple of times at work she noticed Matron looking at her with concern.

'Are you eating enough, nurse?' she asked once. 'Only you've lost a lot of weight lately. Your face is looking drawn. Is caring for these soldiers taking its toll? Do you want a few days off?'

'No!' she said, knowing the worst thing she could do would be to moulder around at home with nothing to occupy her mind. 'I'll be fine.'

Her mother was worried too, and occasionally tried to cheer her up, but she seemed to have other things on her mind. The atmosphere at home was frostier than ever, with her parents barely speaking to each other. Mealtimes were excruciating, the painful silence only broken by requests for the salt to be passed, or the jug of water. She was used to the difficult relationship between them. Her father worked too hard and her mother drank too much but she could never work out which was the cause of the other. And now she didn't have the energy or the capacity to concern herself with their problems. So, she simply ignored the situation, thinking it would blow over as numerous other difficulties had in the past. She would work late at the hospital or spend her evenings with Sharmila to avoid being at home.

After several weeks she knew there was no point waiting for a letter anymore. There was no let-up in the constant stream of casualties arriving at the hospital. She threw herself into the work and was gratified when she saw a smile on a soldier's face, or she was able to ease another's pain.

She avoided Nigel Caldwell as best she could, but it was inevitable that she would have to work with him from time to time. He'd never tried to ask her out again. Perhaps he'd heard rumours that she'd been seeing someone else, or perhaps he'd simply given up. Either way, it was a relief, but she still caught him watching her across the ward sometimes, his eyes lingering on her a little longer than necessary.

She'd completely given up hope of ever hearing from Edward again, when one day Dr Jefford, the surgeon, asked to speak to her. She felt prickles of nerves as she went into his office. He was a remote, autocratic figure, feared by the junior doctors and nurses alike. He'd rarely spoken to her before, and as she knocked on his door, she wondered whether she'd done something wrong.

'Ah, nurse, do come in,' he said, looking up from some papers momentarily. 'Take a seat.'

She sat down and waited for him to finish what he was doing, twisting her hands in her lap nervously. At last he put his papers aside, took off his reading glasses and looked at her.

'I'll come straight to the point, nurse. General Slim has asked us to provide volunteers to man a field hospital for casualties at the front. They no longer have the resources to transport the injured down to the hospitals in the plains. It would mean going up into the hills and working in difficult conditions near the front line. You would need to follow the 14th Army as it advances. It would take both mental and physical strength. I'm asking our younger staff without family commitments first. I already have a number of volunteers. I've heard very good things about your work, Miss Walker and I was wondering if you'd be prepared to volunteer?'

It didn't take her long to decide. This would be just the thing to take her away from the difficult situation at home and to absorb her body and mind completely. She didn't mind being in harm's way either. What did it matter if she was injured or even killed in the line of duty? What did her life matter anyway?

'I'm flattered to be asked, I'll do it, Dr Jefford. Count me in.'

'Thank you, nurse,' he beamed. 'We'll be starting out in a few days' time.'

As she returned down the echoing corridor to the ward, another thought entered her mind. They would be going up into the Naga Hills. She had no idea where, but would there be a chance that they might pass through some of the villages that Edward had visited? And if they did, would any of the villagers be able to tell her what had happened to him?

9

Nagabhari, India, 1985

The rickshaw dropped Iris outside the front gate and she approached the door of the bungalow across the scrunching gravel. It looked just as it had in the forties, only the plants growing over the porch were mature and prolific now and there were more pots of geraniums on the veranda. She went up the steps to the front porch, her heart in her mouth. She was about to knock as she used to in the old days, but saw that there was a bell here now, on a chain. She tugged at it and heard a tinkling in the back of the house somewhere. After a minute or two came the shuffling of feet inside and bolts on the door being drawn back. A hunched over old man opened it. His hair was white and he peered at Iris from behind heavy glasses. Behind the wrinkles the face looked familiar. Could it possibly be the same bearer who used to open the door in the old days?

'Kabir?' she asked, incredulous.

'Madam?'

'I'm Iris. Iris Walker as was. I used to come here when I was young. To see Sharmila. Does she still live here?'

The old man's face was instantly wreathed in smiles.

'Oh, madam, come in. Welcome indeed.'

He held the door open wide and she stepped into the hallway. It had changed very little in forty years. The same marble floor, the same heavy bookcase on the wall, filled with volumes of Shakespeare and other great works of English literature; the same steps down to the living room. A low settee had replaced the scatter cushions though, she noted with a smile.

'Can I offer you a drink? Tea perhaps? A cold drink?'

'That's kind, but I won't stop. I take it that Sharmila still lives here?'

'Oh yes, madam. She is still living here. Her husband, Professor Deepak died a few years ago, but she is still here. But she is not here today, I'm afraid,' he said, shaking his head. 'She has gone for two or three days to stay with her daughter in Benares. She will be back on Friday.'

'Thank you. Could you tell her I called and that I'd love to call on her again if she's happy to see me? I'm staying at the Lake View Hotel.'

The old man bowed. 'Of course. I will tell her. And we will telephone your hotel when she is back.'

'Thank you,' she said, preparing to leave.

'It is very nice to see you again, madam,' the old man said bowing his head again. 'You were a very good friend to memsahib during the war.'

As she walked across the drive back to the rickshaw, she reflected on what he'd said. She *had* been a good friend to Sharmila in those days, and Sharmila had been a good friend to her too. But she'd not lived up to the expectations of friendship. Guilt ran through her as it always did as she thought of

Sharmila and how they'd stopped writing after a few years. How had life treated her since then?

She asked the rickshaw-wallah to take her back to the hotel. She hadn't told Elspeth she was going out, and felt she should check on her before going further afield. But when they reached the end of Sharmila's road, she asked him to take a detour down Hospital Road. She wanted to see if the old building was still standing. As it came into view round a bend, her spirits sank. Like the Residence and Elspeth's old home, it appeared derelict and abandoned. The front gates were chained together and the cobbled drive full of weeds. The white painted walls of the hospital itself were peeling, mould staining the lower floors. The windows were boarded up, weeds were growing from the drains and gutters and the balcony that used to run the length of the first floor was covered in rust and collapsing in places. As they passed the gates, she had an image of herself rushing out of the front entrance to meet Edward, parked up on the drive in the maharajah's car.

'Old British hospital not used anymore,' the rickshaw-wallah remarked over his shoulder. 'New hospital on edge of town. Much better, much cleaner.'

'I'm sure,' she said, but felt a pang of sadness for the old building where she'd spent so many hours caring for injured soldiers. It was as if a part of her past had been taken from her.

Elspeth sounded a little brighter when Iris knocked on her door and, when she entered, Elspeth was sitting up in bed. She'd brushed her hair and there was colour in her cheeks.

'Feeling better?'

'A little bit. But I think I should stay in the hotel today. I don't want to tempt fate.'

'Of course. I just came to check you were OK,' Iris said, sitting down in one of the armchairs.

'Where have you been?'

'Well...' she was about to tell her that she'd been to Sharmila's house, but then thought better of it. She had a shrewd idea that Elspeth's views on her friendship with an Indian girl would be similar to Delphine's. 'I just got the rickshaw-wallah to take me for a drive...' Elspeth was frowning at her. 'We passed the old city hospital actually, where I used to work.'

'Really?'

'Yes. It's so sad. It's gone to rack and ruin like so many of the old buildings.'

Elspeth pulled a face and shuddered. 'I never knew how you could work there. All those injured men. I couldn't have borne it.'

'It was hard sometimes, but they were understaffed so it wouldn't have been fair to leave.'

'And you went up into the hills, didn't you? With that wretched field hospital. I don't know how you could have stood that.'

Iris shrugged. 'By then I was used to it.'

'And that chappie went with you too, didn't' he? That young doctor chappie. Nigel Caldwell.'

'I didn't know you knew Nigel,' Iris said, surprised.

'I didn't know him well. He used to come to the club sometimes,' then a sly look crept into Elspeth's eyes. 'He was sweet on you, wasn't he?'

'Oh, I don't know about that!' Iris replied, wondering how on earth Elspeth knew anything about that, and why she'd remembered it from so long ago.

'That poor young fellow,' Elspeth said, her eyes suddenly far away. 'What people suffered back then!'

10

Nagabhari, India, March 1944

The plane that was going to take them into the hills was an old Dakota Douglas transport plane. Iris had imagined they would be going up on horseback or in bullock carts. In her mind's eye, they would wind through the jungle on a narrow track, passing through Naga villages on the way. She might even have a chance to ask some of the locals if they'd seen Edward and his party.

It simply hadn't entered her head that they would fly, but when she reported with her suitcase to the hospital before dawn on the morning they were due to leave, Dr Jefford said, 'Your aircraft is ready and waiting on the airstrip outside town. There are four of you making the trip. I've ordered a taxi to take you out there.'

'Aircraft?'

'Indeed. Have you flown before, nurse?'

She shook her head, swallowing, digesting this development.

'Well, it's quite straightforward. These RAF pilots make

that trip into the mountains all the time. There's nothing to worry about.'

She was surprised to see Nigel Caldwell amongst the other volunteers. There were also two young nurses from another ward whom she barely knew. They all crammed into the taxi and no one spoke as it ferried them through the old town, where shopkeepers were just opening up and sweepers were sluicing the pavements clean before the business of the day began. Iris wondered vaguely when she would see the place again, but it didn't bother her too much. Nothing bothered her much nowadays; she was even indifferent to her own fate.

But, despite that indifference, when she first caught sight of the aircraft from the window of the taxi, her stomach began to churn with nerves. It was an ungainly looking, rather battered propellor plane, painted in striped camouflage colours of khaki and dark green; it looked as though it had been in a few battles itself. The side door stood open, and wooden crates were being loaded on by some Indian troops.

The taxi stopped beside the plane and they all got out and stood rather awkwardly on the runway.

'Do you know where we're going?' she asked Nigel.

'A place called Imphal. It's on a plateau up in the hills. It's basically under siege by the Japs. A lot of the wounded are evacuated from there to hospitals like ours, but not everyone can be. Some are too badly wounded and others are suffering from malaria and typhus and would die on the flight. So, the field hospital up there patches up the worst casualties and gets them ready for evacuation and nurses those who need to stay.'

Once the boxes and equipment were loaded, a sergeant beckoned the four of them forward. They had to scramble onto the aircraft via the loading door; the soldiers had put orange crates out to act as steps. Inside the aircraft there was so much cargo that there was virtually no space, and there were certainly no seats.

'You'll just have to find yourselves somewhere to perch,' the sergeant barked, then slammed the door shut.

Iris crouched down in a narrow gap between one of the crates and the fuselage, beneath a window. She held onto some webbing attached to the wall of the aircraft. Her heart was hammering as the engines spluttered into life and the plane began to taxi. She looked around at the faces of the other volunteers and they were as white and fearful as she knew her own was. The engines reached deafening volume and through the floor she could feel the throb of them and sense the speed of the aircraft as it gathered pace down the runway. Then with a soft bump they were airborne and rising quickly towards the Naga Hills. She looked out of the window and gasped in wonder as they banked and turned and she could see the whole of Nagabhari beneath them. There was the main street, the covered market, the university, her own home, then they were flying out over the lake and above the domes, parapets and gardens of the Lake Palace. It looked like a doll's house spread out like that beneath her. Seeing it made her think of Edward and how he had looked at her that very first evening. A wave of sadness washed through her as they left the palace behind and headed away from the town.

The propellers settled into a monotonous thrumming as they rose towards the jungle covered hills, and soon the aircraft was flying above them and heading up into the clouds. The plane rocked and swayed as it entered the clouds and Iris' heart lurched. She'd not expected this. She felt the remaining blood drain from her face and she turned towards Nigel.

'It's alright. This is normal. There are always wind currents inside the clouds,' he said, seeing her ashen face.

After a few minutes they made it out through the top of

the clouds and were looking down on them, still climbing. Her fear instantly forgotten, her heart soared at the sight of the extraordinary beauty all around. The sky was bright blue and the clouds were spread beneath them like a fluffy white blanket. She watched, fascinated, as the shadow of the plane scudded across the bright surface. Sometimes there were breaks in the cloud cover and then she got an uninterrupted panorama of the mountains beneath. Layers and layers of them, blue with mist in the distance, stretching as far as the eye could see, covered in jungle, an occasional river snaking through them, or a clearing dotted with the huts of a mountain village. Again, she thought of Edward. Whatever had become of him? Was he still down there somewhere?

After forty or fifty minutes flying at that altitude, the plane began to descend. They bumped back down through the clouds and as they emerged, all around them were the peaks of the Naga Hills. The plane plunged on down, between two peaks, scudding over the tops of the teak trees in the jungle, and in a few minutes an area of flat land came into sight, surrounded by jungled mountains. In the middle was a group of buildings, but surrounding them was acre upon acre of tents, stores and military vehicle parks. In minutes they were heading for the runway, then, with a bump they landed on the grass strip, the brakes came on and the plane screeched to a halt, then immediately turned and began taxiing away. Iris clung on to the hessian strap for dear life but even so was thrown from side to side, banging against the fuselage one second, a wooden crate the next.

The next second they were at a standstill, the side door was flung open and a military voice barked.

'Everyone out, double quick. We need to unload the ammunition and explosives right away.'

So, they'd been travelling with crates of ammunition. It

didn't surprise Iris, after all, they had just flown into the epicentre of a battle.

She unwound herself from the strap, stood up and stretched her aching limbs, then followed Nigel to the edge of the aircraft where she had to jump down.

As she'd seen from the air, they'd landed in a sea of canvas. Row upon row of military tents stretched in every direction.

An officer approached. 'Are you the medical volunteers? Follow me.' He turned on his heel and plunged into a passage between two marquees. Iris struggled along behind him with her suitcase, wishing she'd packed fewer clothes, the others following behind, until they emerged onto a patch of grass in front of a tent marked 'Field Hospital'.

'This is where you'll be working, but I'll take you to your billets first.' And once again he set off briskly down a narrow passage between the hospital tent and its neighbour, leaving them to follow as best they could.

The tent he took them to was bigger than Iris had expected and when they looked inside they saw that the floor was made out of bamboo and was raised about a foot off the ground. It meant that they had to step up when they entered.

'That's because of the rats,' said the officer peremptorily. 'You each have a camp bed with a mosquito net. There's a wash tent behind. You'll be well looked after here. There are cooks, water carriers, beasties to empty the thunder boxes, dhobi-wallahs for your laundry. That tent over there is a dining tent, and the one behind it is a sort of mess for medical officers. There are a few armchairs and books in there if you're interested. Make yourselves comfortable, then report back to the field hospital. They need you to start work straight away. Now, Doctor Caldwell, let me show you to your billet. It's just across here.'

Two of the camp beds were placed side by side, with

another one on the opposite wall of the tent. Iris offered to take that one and the two other girls thanked her. They told her their names were Ellen and Mary. They had come out to India together and had nursed in the same ward in the Nagabhari hospital ever since.

'It's good that we were both accepted as volunteers,' said Mary. 'We wanted to stay together.'

Iris smiled, it was good to see how close these two friends were, but it made her think that she would probably have to face a lot of this alone.

'Why did you volunteer?' asked Ellen. Iris shrugged.

'I needed to get away from home and I wanted to do something to help,' she replied simply. She wasn't going to tell them about Edward and how pining for him had made her low and vulnerable, and reckless about her own survival.

They took it in turns to wash in the small bathroom tent, which consisted of a basin and a bucket of cold water, changed into their nurses' uniforms, then made their way back through the forest of tents to the field hospital.

As they stepped inside, Iris took in a sharp breath of astonishment. The tent was enormous, white canvas with a vaulted roof. There were three sections, crudely separated from each other by canvas curtains. It was filled with row upon row of camp beds, all occupied by sick or injured men. A matron bustled up as they entered. Her face showed the strain of overwork and the traumatic conditions.

'You must be the volunteers from Nagabhari hospital. I'm so pleased you're here, girls. We're very short staffed and men are coming in by field ambulance from the front all the time, twenty-four hours per day in fact. Now you can each take a section of the ward. The men in this front section need water and their wounds dressed. Dressings and equipment are over there on that trestle table.'

So, for the rest of the day, Iris removed dressings, cleaned wounds and dressed them with fresh bandages. She mopped sweating brows and gave thirsty men water. She was used to these tasks, but she noticed that these men had even worse wounds than the ones who made it down to the city hospital and she remembered what Nigel had told her; these men weren't suitable for evacuation. She guessed that many of them would die of their injuries here on the Imphal plain, so far from home.

That night, she collapsed, exhausted, onto her camp bed after a basic supper of mutton and rice in the dining tent. As she began to drift off to sleep she noticed a sound which she then realised had been ever present throughout the day. It was the rumbling of explosions and the ack-ack of machine-gun fire and it came from high up in the hills. She sat up, alarmed. She hadn't realised the enemy was that close. She looked at the other two girls, who hadn't yet put out their hurricane lamps.

'Do you hear that?' Ellen said, her eyes wide with fear. 'It's the fighting. Do you think the Japs will invade the camp?'

Iris had no answer. It was what she was secretly fearing herself. But before she could say anything, the curtain of the tent was pulled back and Nigel put his head round.

'Excuse me, ladies. Sorry to butt in, but I meant to tell you. Don't worry about the gunfire. There are skirmishes up in the hills and there's no chance of it coming down here. The Japs are trying to take several vantage points up there, at the moment they're at Sangshak, a village on the ridge. But our men are holding them off.'

'How do you know all this?' asked Iris.

'I was chatting with the CO over dinner. So there's no need to worry. Sleep well.'

Slightly relieved and reassured by his words, Iris settled

down under the mosquito net, and in her exhausted state, sleep came very quickly.

Over the next few days, the pressure on the ward increased. Men appeared from the battlegrounds on a variety of types of transport, some were stretchered in by hand, others on bullock carts or some came by field ambulance. Aided by Nigel, the Military Officer assessed them quickly. The majority were sent to the runway to await an airlift to a permanent hospital further afield. Others, who needed immediate attention, were taken into the hospital tent where the doctors would perform emergency operations in a cordoned off rear section of the tent. They would then be cared for on the ward.

Iris worked tirelessly for long hours alongside the other nurses; Matron and Joan, another volunteer who'd been there when they arrived, and her two new friends, Ellen and Mary. She had nothing but respect for everyone working there. They all gave of their best in difficult conditions and no one ever complained. Although they had time off, they were normally so exhausted, they fell straight to sleep. So, her entire life consisted of working and sleeping. At night, the only thing keeping them awake was the rumble of gunfire from the hills and the rats scrabbling under the tent.

Iris didn't mind the work or the conditions. It took her mind off the trauma of losing Edward. Gradually, over time, the pain of not knowing what had happened to him lessened. Her hopes of getting out into the villages to ask if anyone had seen Edward were dashed. Imphal was surrounded by jungle covered hills and the enemy occupied many of the hilltop positions. There was no hope of leaving except by aircraft.

The men they were nursing were of many different nationalities: British, Indian, Burmese, Nepalese, and even some Naga tribesmen. Each nationality had their own separate sections of the tent because their dietary requirements were all different and the cooks had a complicated job making sure Hindus weren't given beef, Muslims had no pork, and Buddhists were only offered vegetarian food.

Iris was fascinated by the Naga tribesmen, who came in wearing traditional dress and carrying spears. Most of them spoke no English, but after a few days, one arrived who did speak a few, stumbling words. He had sustained a serious stomach wound and was heavily sedated for the first few days, but one day, while Iris was changing his dressing, he opened his eyes and said, quite clearly, 'Thank you, nurse.'

When he was well enough to hold a conversation, she asked him gently whether he'd ever heard of a village called Nangtek. It was the address Edward had scribbled on the paper he'd handed her before leaving, and where she'd written to him, post restante.

'Yes. I know the village,' the tribesman said.

'I'm looking for a friend who I know went there a few months ago.' From her pocket she fished out the picture of Edward and showed it to the warrior. He screwed up his eyes and peered at it. She thought his eyes widened for a second, but he passed the photograph back to her, shaking his head.

'I not know this man. Very rare for white men go to villages.'

'Are you sure?' she asked. She wasn't quite convinced that he was telling her the truth. 'He was there with a couple of colleagues. Englishmen. One had a long beard.'

He shook his head again, vehemently this time. 'I not know him,' he said and the finality of his tone told her that the questioning was at an end.

After that, she showed the picture to every Naga warrior she nursed but they all had the same reaction. It was puzzling. Most of them admitted to knowing the village of Nangtek, but none of them had seen Edward or his party.

As the days wore on, alarming rumours of losses in the mountains filtered down to the field hospital. The villages of Sangshak and Ukhrul fell to the Japanese with many British casualties, and the Japanese blocked the mountain road between Imphal and Kohima, cutting off the strategically important village of Kohima and putting Imphal itself under threat.

Every day, more allied troops arrived by plane into Imphal; Dakota transport planes were landing and taking off every few minutes. The valley was now even more crowded with tents housing several regiments, and additional supplies were airdropped by parachute. It became hazardous to walk out in the open if a plane was flying overhead; you risked being hit by a crate of food or ammunition.

One morning, during the build-up of troops, a British officer came to talk to the medical staff. They gathered outside the tent for a briefing.

'General Slim has ordered non-combatants to be airlifted out of Imphal. Only fighting troops can be stationed here from now on. We'll need to evacuate the hospital and all the staff down to the hospital at Comilla.'

Matron stepped forward. 'A lot of the sick men won't last the journey, Colonel.'

'We'll have to do our best for them, Matron. The situation here is critical as I'm sure you're aware. V-Force – our men on the ground behind Jap lines, tell us that a Japanese push for Imphal is imminent. So, we'll be shipping you all out without delay, beginning this afternoon. But I have a separate mission for a couple of medical staff. It is not without its risk and discomfort and whoever volunteers will need to be aware of that.'

'Go on, Colonel,' said Matron and Iris looked around at

the faces of the other volunteers. All were looking down at their shoes. All apart from Nigel.

'We will still need some medical relief on the ground behind the front line. We're establishing a field hospital near Tamu, just behind the fighting. Like here at Imphal, wounded men will need patching up before they can be evacuated, and there are those who are too ill to be moved. But the conditions will be basic, and it is only a stone's throw from the front line. Is anyone prepared to take that risk?'

'I am,' Iris spoke up before she'd had a chance to think too carefully about it. Drawing a blank about Edward with the Naga tribesmen had finally convinced her that she would never see him again. She now had even less reason to worry about her own survival.

'That's very brave of you, nurse,' said the colonel. 'Anyone else?'

There was an embarrassed pause and some shuffling of feet. Then someone spoke.

'I'll go too.' It was Nigel. Iris looked up into his eyes and saw something shining there. Was it determination and bravery? She wasn't sure.

11

The journey up into the hills this time was in a bi-plane - a 'moth'- which was smaller and slightly more comfortable than the Dakota, though for Iris at least, the whole trip was tinged with fear at what awaited them at the front. Iris and Nigel sat in bucket seats side by side behind the pilot. The plane took off from the airstrip at Imphal and ascended steeply over the encircling mountains. To Iris, peering out of the window, the aircraft seemed to brush the tops of the jungle trees as it climbed. As they flew over the mountain ridge above Imphal, Nigel pointed out a straggling line of trenches where British troops were dug in. Occasionally, they caught sight of a burst of gunfire, an area of scrub on fire or a burning hut. It was terrifying to Iris that out there, on those mountain tops, in those exposed conditions in the mud and the jungle, men were dying.

This plane flew at a lower altitude than the Dakota, barely skimming the tree tops, and in less than an hour the pilot announced they were about to descend.

'Hold on to your seats, this is a tight landing.'

They descended above the treetops until Iris thought they

must actually be clipping the branches, then suddenly the trees came to an abrupt end and the plane dropped sharply. They landed within a few yards on a bumpy grass strip carved out of the jungle. As the plane taxied to a stop, Iris realised that her legs had turned to jelly.

An eccentric-looking officer with pebble glasses wearing khaki shorts and a pith helmet ran up to greet them.

'I'm Doc Bourne. Medical Officer here. I'm glad you've come,' he said, pumping their hands enthusiastically. 'We're pretty understaffed here, just me and a couple of orderlies, so you are very welcome. Very welcome indeed. I'll show you round.'

Iris was uncomfortably aware of the constant sound of shelling and gunfire that punctuated the air. It was so loud that when a shell exploded, the ground under her feet shook.

'How close is the front, actually?' she asked.

'Oh, fifty yards or so over in that direction,' Dr Bourne waved his arm in the direction of a thin line of trees and as she looked, Iris could tell that those straggly specimens must have once been surrounded by others, which had obviously been ripped out and destroyed by the shelling.

'We're quite safe tucked away back here though. They'll let us know if there's any chance of the Japs breaking through the lines.'

'That's reassuring,' she muttered.

He led them through the trees towards a group of tents and as they walked towards them, two men staggered into view supporting a third on their shoulders. The third man looked to be in a bad way, blood streaming from his forehead.

'Casualties come to us day and night,' said Dr Bourne, 'The fighting never stops,' then he turned to the soldiers. 'This way, lads, bring him inside the tent. The orderlies will help you. I'll be along in a minute.'

He showed Iris and Nigel to two small canvas tents in the same clearing as the hospital tent. Iris saw that they were on the edge of a great forest of tents.

'Those are for the troops,' Dr Bourne explained.

'Conditions are quite rudimentary here, I'm afraid. There's a trench toilet behind that bamboo screen, which is dug daily, and we have a canvas bath you can use if you want to bathe. The bearers will bring you water for it if you ask, but water is very short up here so we have to limit ourselves.'

Iris pulled back the opening of her tent and inside the stifling interior was nothing but a camp bed with a mosquito net and a groundsheet. There was no bamboo platform here and she shuddered when she thought of the rats scrabbling around under the floor at Imphal.

'You're on your own in there, I'm afraid, Nurse Walker, but Doctor Caldwell and the orderlies are only next door, so you needn't worry. Now, if you'd like to pop your case inside the tent, we need you on the ward right away.'

She did as he suggested and followed him to the hospital tent, gasping at the heat and the smell of putrefaction as she stepped inside. This was much more cramped and rudimentary than the field hospital at Imphal. Men were lying on stretchers and camp beds with no space between them. She sensed that many were mortally injured.

'This ward is for those too badly injured to make it out of here,' explained Dr Bourne. 'We also have typhus and malaria patients in the next tent on. Most of them have light injuries but are too ill to be evacuated.'

The air was filled with groans and sobs of men in pain. There was only one man smiling; an impossibly young-looking lad with a bandage around his head.

'Hello, doc,' he said jauntily to Dr Bourne as they passed.

'Hello, Jimmy,' the doctor replied, then when they were

out of earshot he said, 'Young Jimmy is an inspiration to us all. He refuses to let what's happened to him get him down. He had a gunshot wound to the skull, but keeps smiling nevertheless.'

'What would you like us to do?' asked Nigel.

'Well, perhaps you could take a look at the casualty who's just come in, doctor, then I have a couple of amputations waiting, so could you assist me with those. Nurse Walker, could you go into the malaria tent and administer medication. It's all laid out on a trolley just inside. Two pills per man.'

The malaria tent was quieter than the other ward but no less crowded. Most of the men in there appeared either unconscious or asleep. Their pale faces glistened with sweat in the dim light and many were twisting and turning on their beds, delirious with fever. Iris began at one end, doling out the malaria pills, holding up a cup of water to each man. Most were grateful, trying to force a smile, others barely woke when she shook them, and hardly acknowledged her presence.

When she'd finished she returned to the main tent and the doctor asked her to check the men's' dressings and change those who needed it. This was familiar territory for Iris, but she was shocked by the extent of the injuries these men had sustained and by the look in their eyes. To a man they seemed dazed and defeated, a magnified version of the look she'd seen on soldiers in Imphal and at the city hospital.

Only Jimmy was chirpy and conversational as she removed his bandage, revealing many crude stitches on his shaved head. While she cleaned the area, he asked her where she was from and told her he came from Kent and couldn't wait to get back to see his sweetheart.

Later, as the sun went down over the jungle, Iris sat with Nigel, Dr Bourne and the two orderlies at a trestle table in the clearing and were served a supper of tough meat and apple puree.

'What meat is this?' Iris asked, chewing.

'It's mule, I'm afraid,' Dr Bourne replied. 'The animals are used to haul supplies up the mountain and when they've done their bit that way, we slaughter them and use their meat.'

In the morning when she awoke just after dawn, Iris immediately sensed something was different. Sitting up in bed she realised. Although she could hear gunfire, it wasn't so loud. She got dressed quickly and as she stepped out of her tent, she saw Nigel coming out of his. At that moment an officer came running up to tell them that British troops had recaptured the ridge immediately behind the camp and the battle had moved on along the mountain top.

'There are still injured men out on the ridge,' he said. 'I'm going with stretcher bearers to recover them, but I could do with some medical assistance. Some of them might not make it back here without it.'

'I'll go,' Iris said immediately.

Nigel stepped forward. 'I don't think you should. I can go.'

'No, I insist. There's no reason why I shouldn't help,' she said.

'Alright,' he said reluctantly. 'We'll go together.'

'This way then, follow me,' the officer said and plunged into the remains of the forest that separated the camp from the battleground.

As they walked between the thin line of straggly teak trees and the battlefield came into view, what Iris saw there took the breath from her body. Beyond the trees, the mountain top was denuded of vegetation. It was a churned-up sea of mud, scarred by deep trenches that snaked around the hilltop. Bodies were strewn everywhere. Japanese, Indian, Burmese, Nepalese and British. Many must have lain there sometime as they were bloated and some were heaving with maggots. There were bloody body parts too, lying in the mud. Amongst the men lay several dead mules, their distended stomachs huge against the blue sky. The stench of rotting flesh was overpowering, and Iris felt her stomach heave. She turned away and took a deep breath.

'Go back,' Nigel said his arm around her shoulder. 'You look as though you're going to faint. You shouldn't have come.'

'No,' she insisted, fighting against the nausea. 'You need help. Some of these men might be alive.'

'Alright,' he said, reluctance in his voice. 'But I don't want you fainting on me.'

They went from body to body, listening for a heartbeat, feeling for a pulse. Some were so obviously dead, flies buzzing around congealed wounds, that they quickly moved onto the next one. They found three men still alive. Nigel performed emergency first-aid on them, then the stretcher bearers loaded them gently on to bamboo stretchers and carried them carefully back to the field hospital. Doctor Bourne shook his head when he saw them.

'This terrible war,' he said quietly.

Iris assisted him and Nigel as they worked on the men, giving them injections of adrenaline, fixing up saline drips. One man had been bayoneted, his intestines perforated, another's lower legs had been smashed by a shell and the third had been shot in the chest.

She watched the doctors as they worked tirelessly to help these men and she realised that she had a new, creeping respect for Nigel. He didn't have to be here. He could have been evacuated to Comilla alongside the rest of the staff at the hospital, but he'd put himself in harm's way to use his skills to help these dying men.

'We need to operate on all three,' Dr Bourne said. 'We'll

remove the bullet from this lad's chest first. That will be quickest and he has the best chance of survival. Nigel, you'd better scrub up.'

Through the long day, the two doctors operated on the three men and Iris assisted. She had no time to feel nauseous, and she knew that the men's' lives depended on her being calm, so she sterilised equipment, sutured and sewed up wounds and cleaned and dressed them. Despite their best efforts, by the evening the two more seriously wounded men had died but the one with the gunshot wound was still breathing.

'It was worth it then,' said Nigel as they sat down at the table for their evening meal. 'At least we managed to preserve one life today. It makes all this worthwhile.'

As they chewed their way through their second meal of mule steak and apple puree, Iris asked him what had made him want to become a doctor.

'It was my father, really,' he said. 'He was a coalminer, and he suffered an injury at work. His legs were crushed in the accident so he was a cripple from my early childhood. The local doctor used to come round and do what he could to ease his pain. The doctor was so patient, so cheerful. His visits used to give my father a pick-up that went way beyond the physical. So, I decided then, that's what I wanted to do.'

As he spoke she saw the enthusiasm shining in his quiet, grey eyes.

'That must have been a lot of work,' she said.

'Yes, and my family had no money,' he said, smiling. 'That same doctor helped me get a scholarship to a good school and to later on get into medical school. He was such an inspiration to me.'

'And what made you come out to India?'

'My father died and my mother passed away too. I thought

it was time to see the world. I came to India just before war broke out. And what about you?'

'Oh, I was born in India. In Hyderabad actually. My father was posted there. But when I was little he was transferred to Nagabhari. He's been Resident there ever since.'

'So, you don't feel England is your home?'

'Not really, no. I went back to school and to study in London, but I've always felt more at home here in India.'

As they were speaking, an officer approached the table and called Dr Bourne away to speak to him. When he returned, his forehead was pulled up in an anxious frown.

'That was a message from the Commanding Officer. They've had intelligence from V-Force about the next strategic strike from the Japs. They are moving some troops along the ridge a few miles away. They want us to go with them.'

'What about the patients?' Iris asked, alarmed.

'They'll have to be transported by truck or cart. It's happened before, but I expect some of them won't make it. We're leaving at dawn.'

Later, as she lay under her mosquito net, before sleep overcame her, she thought of the injustice of it all. All those poor men in the hospital tents, little more than boys, who'd survived the battle and were hanging onto life by a thread. Tomorrow, they would be put in jeopardy again, not by the Japanese, but by the journey to a new camp. It seemed ironic, somehow.

12

E arly in the morning, just after dawn, two army trucks arrived in the hospital clearing, followed shortly afterwards by two large and lumbering bullock carts. The stretcher bearers quickly got to work carrying men from their camp beds in the tents out to the transport. Iris tried to make sure each patient was as comfortably stowed as he could be and to explain to them what was happening. Most of the men were bewildered to be blinking awake to a new day, only to be whisked from the safety of the tent out into the rising heat of the exposed mountaintop.

The most critical patients were travelling first. The two doctors were to ride with them on one of the army trucks. Once they had left, a group of soldiers began to dismantle the tents. They loaded them onto a smaller truck which went off to the new site to be set up there before the first patients arrived.

Iris travelled on the second army truck. She sat up front with the driver. They were soon out of the clearing and travelling through the thick, dark jungle which quickly closed in around them. The road was just a rough, mud track, recently hewn out of the trees, and the truck often skidded and slid on the slippery surface. Iris got a sense of just how dense the jungle was here and how far removed this place was from civilisation. It struck her as strange that the armies of two great foreign empires were meeting here to fight it out over this remote, forgotten terrain.

When they arrived at the new camp, another few miles along the ridge, the first hospital tent had already been erected. As Iris got down from the cab, she heard the rumble of shelling and gunfire loud and clear, even louder than it had been on the first night. Two stretcher bearers were already hard at work unloading patients from the first army truck and ferrying them into the tent. The sun was high in the sky and the air clammy and hot.

Iris went inside the tent and joined Nigel and Dr Bourne who were moving between the camp beds, giving the men water, trying to make sure each man was as comfortable as he could be. Iris was dismayed at the effect this short but disruptive journey had had. Many of the men looked even paler and sicker than before.

When she reached Jimmy's bed, she was shocked to see him lying back on the thin pillow, a pained expression on his usually cheerful face. It was drained of colour, and beads of sweat stood out on his brow.

'Jimmy, are you OK? Do you want some water?' she asked, kneeling down beside him. His eyes flickered open and he forced a wan smile.

'Hello, nurse,' he whispered. 'Yes please.'

She held a cup to his parched lips and he sipped weakly, a lot of it dribbling down his chin. Then he closed his eyes, as if the effort of lifting his head to drink had exhausted him. Iris beckoned Dr Bourne over.

'Jimmy looks to be in a bad way,' she said. The doctor shook his head and took out his stethoscope.

'I'll examine him and do what I can, but it's patients like Jimmy who will have suffered most by being moved.'

Reluctantly, she left him and moved on to the next patient. All the time, the stretcher bearers were bringing more men in from the second army vehicle and the tent was getting hotter and more crowded by the minute. When Iris went outside for a breath of air, she was shocked to hear, amongst the rattle of gunfire, the drone of an engine approaching above the jungle. Were the Japanese attacking the camp by air? She was about to take cover when an aircraft burst into view, a rope from its fuselage dangling an enormous crate which swung to and fro dangerously. Iris immediately recognised it as a supply drop and stood well clear as the crate careered to the ground in the middle of the clearing, narrowly missing one of the army trucks.

Two soldiers rushed to the crate and carried it back nearer the tents. She watched them prise the wood apart. It was already splintered from the fall and came away easily. Then they began to remove packages and she could see from the labels that it contained bandages, dressings, bottles of chloroform and other medicines.

'Dr Bourne will be pleased,' she said to the soldiers. One of them beamed, holding up another package; a box of tins.

'And so will everyone else. This is bully beef. It will make a change from mule for supper!'

The rest of the day was spent settling the men, distributing medicines and supervising their mealtimes. In the afternoon, two men with serious injuries gave up the fight and breathed their last. They were removed from the tent by the orderlies, who took them to the edge of the compound to be buried. Iris watched them cross the clearing from the doorway of the tent, then she saw Nigel standing under a teak tree smoking a cigarette. She went across to speak to him and was shocked to see how haggard his face looked, the troubled look in his eyes.

'It's all so futile,' he said, taking a long drag of the cigarette. 'We work so hard to save them, then an order comes through from the CO that drives a coach and horses through our efforts.'

'I know,' said Iris, lighting up a cigarette herself. 'The journey has had a terrible effect on some of the men. It's so distressing.'

'Sometimes I wonder what we're here for,' he said grimly.

'Oh, don't say that! Our work here is so valuable. So many more would have died without it. We need to hold on to the positives.'

He was silent for a time, dragging on his cigarette and staring into the distance.

'I know, you're right,' he said suddenly, throwing the stub of his cigarette down and grinding it into the mud with his heel. 'Thank you for listening to me. I'm so thankful that you're here.'

That evening they ate the bully beef at the trestle table set up outside the tent. Two officers came to join them from the nearby army camp and told them how the fighting was fierce but how the 14th Army was pushing the Japanese back from the ridge gradually. After the meal, as the officers left to go back to their camp, Iris spotted a tall man slipping out from between the trees to speak to them. He didn't look like a soldier, he was dressed in civilian clothes: a white shirt and canvas trousers. He handed the officer what looked like some papers, then melted back into the trees again.

'Who's that?' she asked Dr Bourne with interest. There had been something that struck a chord with her about that mysterious figure, but she couldn't put her finger on what it was.

'Oh, we're not meant to know about the likes of him,' said the doctor, tapping the side of his nose. 'He's one of our friends from V-Force. They're the army's eyes and ears on the ground in these hills, slipping behind Japanese lines, disrupting their manoeuvres if they can, or just reporting back on what they find out. They are very brave and very valuable.'

That night she dreamed of Edward, and when she awoke, she realised that she had barely thought of him since she'd been working at the front line. Being in constant danger and working as hard as she had been had taken her mind off her sadness. In her dream, he was lying sick on a camp bed in a cavernous room in the Lake Palace. She went into the room to nurse him and as she bent to mop his sweating brow, he sat up, put his arms out and pulled her towards him. She awoke with a start, sitting up in her camp bed, sweating. The sound of gunfire was echoing from the front and she lay back with a deep sigh, knowing sleep would probably elude her until dawn. The dream had brought Edward back vividly; his beautiful eyes, his tousled hair, the feel of his arms around her. It also revived the heartbreak and sadness she'd experienced losing him and she realised it had never been far from the surface, all those weeks she'd been away.

They stayed at that camp for several weeks, while the battle raged on the nearby ridge. Iris got so used to the sound of shelling and gunfire that it barely registered with her anymore. Injured men were brought in every day; the ones with the worst injuries stayed, but some were evacuated down to Comilla. Some of the others recovered and were also evacuated either to convalesce or to be reassigned to their army units. Before they left, they all thanked Iris, the orderlies and the doctors.

'I'll never forget you, nurse,' many of them said and she was touched by those words. She wouldn't forget them either.

But many of them didn't improve, and day by day she saw them slipping away, dying from their wounds, from blood poisoning or from disease. She felt powerless and frustrated that she couldn't do more. She knew that without better medicines and conditions these men would die before her eyes.

One day, Jimmy gave up the struggle and closed his eyes for the last time. Iris herself found him one morning as she came to check on the ward. She knew as soon as she set eyes on him that he was gone. His skin was waxy and translucent, his eyes open, staring blankly up at the canvas roof. Fighting back the tears, she pulled the sheet over his head and went to find one of the doctors. Nigel was in the small tent behind the main one, where they performed operations. He was getting ready for the day ahead.

'What's the matter?' he asked, seeing her face as she entered.

'It's Jimmy,' she said, shaking her head and the tears fell before she had a chance to check them. In a second, Nigel was there in front of her, holding her in his arms. She sobbed on his shoulder. He didn't speak or try to make things better, he just held her, letting her cry herself out. At last the tears were exhausted and he let her go. She stepped back, rubbing the tears away.

'I'm sorry,' she said, but looking up she saw there were tears in Nigel's eyes too.

They buried Jimmy under the trees beside all the others who had died since they'd arrived at the camp. Iris had never visited the graves before, she hadn't felt able; preferring to focus on nursing the living, but this time she felt compelled to go to the funeral Dr Bourne organised for Jimmy. The two orderlies, Nigel, Iris and Dr Bourne stood around the grave while the padre from the nearby army camp read out the words of the funeral service. Afterwards they sang "Dear Lord and Father of Mankind", their thin voices barely audible above the sound of shelling. Afterwards, Jimmy's body, wrapped in a sheet, was lowered into the grave and the orderlies began covering it with earth. Iris couldn't stop the tears from streaming down her cheeks.

'It's such a waste,' she said bitterly to Nigel afterwards as they walked back to the tents. There was no time to grieve properly, they needed to get straight back to work.

'It is. But we need to remember the good things about Jimmy. How much joy he brought to everyone he met.'

The days wore on and gradually the battle moved on along the ridge and the sound of shelling grew fainter.

'We're pushing the Japs back. They're firmly in retreat now,' one of the officers told them at supper one day. 'We'll need to move your camp again in a few days. It's getting too far to bring the wounded now.'

It was true. Whereas before, men had staggered or been carried in straight from the battlefield, now they had to be brought on handcarts or bullock carts. After Dr Bourne had assessed them, some were sent by army vehicle to the airstrip to be evacuated to Comilla, but others, too badly injured to travel, or suffering from disease, stayed in the camp.

'And our intelligence is that the Japs will attack Kohima imminently,' the officer went on. 'We need to have you closer to the front, ready for when it happens.'

So, once again, the next day the camp was packed up and it and all the patients were transported by various means several miles on the bumpy road through the jungle to the new site. This was a patch of desolate ground with barely any trees for cover, just about within sight of the small town of Kohima that was perched on the next ridge.

As she got down from the army truck on arrival, Iris caught sight of a shower of earth spraying in the air from exploding shells. The battle must have already started.

'Are we quite safe here?' she asked the driver, alarmed, and he shrugged. 'It's where the top brass have told you to set up shop, so I'm guessing it must be.'

From where she stood, Iris could just about see the little town spilling down the far hillside, which itself was surrounded by much bigger mountains. The highest building was a white-painted colonial bungalow, set in terraced grounds. Shading her eyes, she could see a tennis court and another building that looked as if it might have been a club. On the outskirts of the town, army camps had been set up. Swathe upon swathe of them, covering the lower terraces. A wave of homesickness swept over her as she looked at the familiar looking buildings, not unlike her own home and the club in Nagabhari. For the first time she longed to be back in Nagabhari in the quiet and safety of her own home.

She tried to put her fears aside and busied herself with making the men comfortable, but the shelling was so loud that everyone was on edge and more than once that afternoon Dr Bourne spoke sharply to her. She left the tent just before the sun went down, going outside for a break. She needed to get away if only for a few minutes. Nigel followed her out.

'Do you want a cigarette?' she asked.

'Of course,' he said. Over the days they'd often taken a smoke break together, chatting about the patients, about the war, their hopes and fears. Now they crossed the ground to the shelter of a couple of forlorn trees near the summit of the ridge.

Iris was just lighting up when she heard the sound of an aeroplane approaching.

'Another supply drop, thank goodness,' she said, but as she

looked up at Nigel's face she saw a flicker of concern in his eyes. She followed his gaze upwards and what she saw shocked her to the core. The engine sound wasn't a lumbering Dakota heading their way, but that of a far lighter, faster aircraft. As it burst into view and dived towards them, in that split second, Iris knew without a shadow of a doubt that it was a Japanese fighter plane.

'Duck,' Nigel yelled, pushing her down beside the tree trunk and diving on top of her. At the same time a burst of machine-gun fire came from the aircraft, then it swooped away. Iris screamed as a searing pain ripped through her back. She'd been hit. She lay back on the ground, unable to move. Then she tried to take a gulp of air but none would come and she tasted fresh blood in her mouth. Nigel was still slumped over her and she needed to get him off her so she could breathe properly. She could barely move, but gradually managed to ease herself out from under him.

Then she heard shouts coming from the direction of the tents and frantic footsteps running towards them.

'Nigel!' she gasped as he slumped on the ground, and she caught sight of the blood oozing from his shattered skull. A wave of nausea swept over her and then everything around her went black.

13

Nagabhari, India, 1985

Iris leaned on the balustrade of her veranda at the Lake View Hotel, looking out over the calm waters of the lake. The sun was at its height, dancing on the ripples on the surface, making them sparkle. Elspeth was resting, so Iris had spent a couple of hours reading her wartime diary, reliving the traumas of nursing at the front during the desperate battles of Imphal and Kohima. Her heart was heavy with sadness and regret for the loss of Nigel. He'd died up there on that scrubby mountain, outside the village of Kohima, gunned down by that Japanese aircraft, and in doing so, he'd saved her own life. She'd often thought about him down the years and regretted how unkind she'd been to him when he'd first asked her out at the city hospital. She'd done her best to avoid him after that and had even been dismayed when he volunteered to go up to Imphal. She'd often wondered whether he might have done that in order to be with her, but had always suppressed that idea as vain and selfish. She preferred to believe that he'd volunteered because he was brave and selfless and had wanted to do his bit for the men suffering and dying for their country.

Now she thought about how the adversity of working at the hospital camp had brought them together and how, over those difficult few weeks, they had grown close. She'd begun to rely on his unfailing calmness, strength and support, and had even enjoyed his quiet, undemanding friendship. She'd often wondered what might have happened had that Japanese Zero aircraft not spotted them smoking together by that tree; a sitting target. Would they have stayed friends? Would they have ever become more than that?

A wave of sadness passed over her. Since returning to Nagabhari, her grief for the loss of Andrew had intensified and she realised that she was mourning not just for him, but for the other men she'd lost in India in her youth; for Edward and for Nigel. Her recent grief had brought these long-forgotten losses to the surface.

She was fingering her garnet pendant, wondering where to go that afternoon to cheer herself up, when the phone beside her bed rang. She ran inside to answer it.

'Iris?'

At first she couldn't place the female voice on the line, but it stirred something in the depths of her memory. She was silent for a few seconds, trying to remember. Then it came to her.

'Sharmila? Is that you?'

'Yes!' the voice was bubbling over with laughter. It sounded just the same even after all these years.

'I happened to phone home and Kabir told me you had called. I was amazed and delighted. What brings you back to India after all this time?'

'Well unfortunately my husband died recently and it seemed the right time to come back.'

'I'm so sorry, Iris. I had no idea.'

'Thank you. It's been over six months, but it's still hard sometimes.'

'I'm sure. Poor you,' Sharmila's voice was full of genuine concern. 'I called to say that I'm coming home tomorrow morning, so would you like to come round in the afternoon?'

'I'd love that, Sharmila,' Iris said, thinking briefly of Elspeth, wondering if she'd be better by then and would be disgruntled at being left alone for the afternoon.

'Alright. Why don't you come at around two then? You know where I am.'

'That's great. I will.... Oh, and Sharmila...'

'Yes?'

'I'm so sorry. That we lost touch. I'm sure it was my fault. It's just...'

'Please don't apologise, Iris. I've always felt guilty about that too. I'm sure it was my fault, not yours. Let's not even mention it again. See you tomorrow afternoon.'

Iris put the phone down, then looking up she was shocked to see Elspeth standing in the doorway, her face like thunder.

'Who was that?' she asked, coming inside and plonking herself down in a cane chair which creaked under her weight.

'Oh, just an old friend,' Iris replied, flustered. 'I thought I would see if she still lived in Nagabhari after all these years and it turns out that she does.'

'And you've made plans to visit her, I hear,' Elspeth said, in a grumpy tone.

'Yes, tomorrow afternoon. I hope you don't mind, only...'

Elspeth drew herself up. 'Is it that Indian girl you used to hang about with? The one married to the academic?'

'Well yes, actually it is,' Iris said, sitting down, astonished that Elspeth had remembered anything about Sharmila, let alone who she'd been married to.

'There was quite a scandal about that young man if I remember correctly,' Elspeth said, a cruel look creeping into her eyes.

'You've got a phenomenal memory I must say, Elspeth. I'd completely forgotten all about it,' she lied, not wanting to get into that subject.

'Yes, there was some mystery about him. Now what was it? Some scandal from his time in Ganpur if I remember rightly...'

'Well, I'm sure it's long forgotten now, whatever it was.'

'And you're seeing her tomorrow afternoon you say?'

'Yes, I hope you don't mind,' Iris said hesitantly, wondering why she was being so deferential to Elspeth. Was she afraid of her temper? 'You could always come too,' she finished weakly.

'No... no. It's alright. My stomach is still not right. My leg's been playing up too. A rest will do me good tomorrow afternoon. In fact, I think I might go back to bed right now.'

Iris heaved a sigh of relief as she watched Elspeth manoeuvre herself and her stick out through the doorway. Then she made herself a cup of tea and returned to the veranda to read more of her diary.

IRIS FELT a touch apprehensive as the rickshaw dropped her off outside Sharmila's bungalow just before two the next afternoon, but as she walked across the drive towards the front door, it flew open and Sharmila appeared smiling broadly. She ran across the veranda and down the steps to greet Iris. They hugged as if the gap of forty years had never happened.

'You look just the same!' Sharmila exclaimed, holding Iris at arm's length.

'I'm not sure about that,' Iris replied, laughing. 'I didn't used to have grey hairs and crows' feet when I was in my twenties. But *you* look marvellous, Sharmila. Even better than when you were young, if that's possible.'

It was true. Sharmila had been a beauty in her youth, but now, in maturity, contentment and happiness shone from her eyes and her smile lit up her face.

'Come on inside,' Sharmila tucked her arm inside Iris' and they went on into the bungalow.

They sat down in the familiar sitting room and Kabir brought them jasmine tea and samosas, just like the old days.

'So,' said Sharmila. 'Tell me all about your life in England. What did you do down the years? Do you have children? Grandchildren?'

'Yes. I have a boy and a girl and four grandchildren now. I see lots of them but none of them lives near me anymore. Oh... and I trained as a teacher when we went home from India.'

'So you didn't stick with nursing?'

Iris shook her head. 'I couldn't face going back to that I'm afraid. Not after the war.'

'Of course. I understand. So, tell me all about it.'

Iris did her best. She told Sharmila how she'd met Andrew, while she was doing her teacher training. He was an archaeologist, working on digs across the country, sometimes travelling abroad. He'd never earned much money but that hadn't mattered to either of them. They'd led a simple life together, full of fun and laughter, and when he'd died suddenly of a heart attack, she'd been devastated.

'What about your children? What do they do?' Sharmila asked.

'Well, Caroline is a teacher like me, and Pete is a surveyor. And they both have two children. A girl and a boy each.'

'How wonderful. I'm so glad you've been happy.'

'And what about you and Deepak?'

Sharmila's face grew wistful. 'Poor Deepak died a few years back now. His health wasn't good as he got older and in the end he had an aneurism. He didn't suffer at all, but it was a big shock.'

'Poor Deepak. I'm so sorry, Sharmila.'

'You know, you were such a support to me when we were young. All those difficult times we went through, all that worrying I did over Deepak.'

'I take it that you got through all that?' Iris asked.

'Yes. Yes, we did. You know, after you'd left for England something changed between us. Suddenly he began to spend more time at home and everything clicked into place. I stopped worrying about him. When our daughter, Nyra was born, he was the perfect father. We never looked back.'

'That's so good to know,' said Iris, remembering those difficult days before she'd left, Sharmila's distress and the part she herself had played in trying to make things better for her friend.

'It's so wonderful that you've finally come back. Have you been sightseeing? Where have you been so far?'

'Well, it's been a bit tricky. I'm travelling with someone else. She also used to live here during the war, but you probably don't know her. Elspeth, her name is. I'm afraid she hasn't been well, but we did get to the Lake Palace on our first day here.'

'The Lake Palace! I'm sorry to say that place has changed rather from when you knew it. Isn't that where you met that gorgeous young man? Edward... wasn't it?'

Iris felt the colour creep into her cheeks. 'Yes. I did meet him there. In fact, I've been thinking a lot about him since I've been here. I've been reading my old diaries. I'd forgotten how much I was affected by him disappearing as he did.'

'Did you ever try to find out what happened to him?'

'I did try writing to the India Office when I got back to England, but drew a complete blank. They couldn't give me any information about his whereabouts, other than that he had worked in Bareilly before the war. I knew that already. So, it's still a mystery I'm afraid. One I doubt will ever be resolved.'

Sharmila fell silent for a few moments, then said, 'What about your parents? Are they still alive?'

'My father died a few years after we went back to England. You know, he never quite recovered from what happened in Nagabhari at the end. It broke him, I'm afraid.'

'I'm so sorry to hear that. Your father was a lovely man.'

'He couldn't settle back in England, seemed like a fish out of water. Mummy is still alive, though. She is in her eighties now and isn't too well. She's in a care home, but she loves to remember India and talk about the old days. It's extraordinary really. She always seemed so unhappy while she was here.'

Sharmila smiled. 'It's funny how the grass is often greener. You know, there aren't many people who remember British rule in Nagabhari, but there is an old man who used to be the chowkidar, or caretaker at the Lake Palace. He lives in the bungalows next door to the old British church. He often sits in his driveway or even on the old church wall. If I ever go past, we have a chat. He loves to talk about the old times and he often mentions your father. You should go and see him. He would love to see a face from back then. I'm sure he would remember you.'

Later, as they said goodbye on the veranda, Sharmila squeezed Iris' hands and said, 'You must come again. We've so much catching up to do. You could bring your friend, maybe?'

Iris laughed. 'Perhaps. She's not the easiest character in the world, but we'll see.'

The light was fading as Iris' rickshaw rattled up the lake-

side road to the hotel and pulled up at the entrance. Iris
thanked the rider and paid him the fare together with a large
tip. She was feeling generous and happy, and she recalled that
that was the way she always felt after spending time with
Sharmila.

She didn't feel like going straight into the hotel, instead,
she wandered out to the shore of the lake to watch the sunset.
It had never failed to enchant her while she lived here, and
now, standing at the water's edge, she remembered how she
and Edward would watch the sky turn dark pink, streaked
with reds and golds as the sun set over the distant hills. She
suddenly felt very close to him again, back in the place where
they'd fallen in love.

With tears in her eyes, she turned and walked back to the
hotel, which was now lit up for the evening, and as she
walked, she saw something that made her stop and blink and
look again. Someone was heading round the side of the building, walking very quickly, without a limp and without a stick.
She followed at a discreet distance, just to make sure she
wasn't hallucinating. The figure walked nimbly up a flight of
steps and made for a side door. The outdoor light above the
door settled any doubts Iris might have had. There was no
mistaking that grey hair and that plaid skirt. The figure
hurrying into the hotel from the side entrance was none other
than Elspeth.

14

Nagabhari, India, 1944

I ris was dimly aware that she'd been asleep for a long, long time. Every time she opened her eyes, exhaustion quickly overcame her, and she was forced to close them and sink back into that voracious sleep that enveloped her whole being. She was also aware that when she did manage to keep her eyes open for more than a couple of seconds, she was staring up at a high, white ceiling, from which were suspended an army of fans whirring round impossibly quickly. The ceiling was familiar, though she'd never seen it from that angle before, but she just couldn't put her finger on where she was.

From time-to-time, faces loomed over her. Anxious eyes peered into hers. Someone put a finger on her eyelid and pulled it back. She blinked the finger away and turned her head to the side. Someone else put a long glass stick in her mouth, then took it out again a while later. Someone else pressed a cold metal object onto her chest. There always seemed to be whispering, panicky voices around her. She could never catch their words, but that didn't bother her. She just wanted to rest, to relax, to sleep for ever.

Then one day she opened her eyes and they stayed open a little longer than before. The drowsiness was wearing off. She looked around and tried to sit up. A searing pain in her shoulder made her gasp and sink back on the pillows.

'Iris, *darling*! Doctor... doctor, she's awake,' she recognised her mother's voice and looking up there was her mother's white face leaning over her, two blue eyes round with surprise.

'Where am I?' Iris muttered, but her mouth couldn't form the words properly. Her mother seemed to understand.

'You're in the hospital. The city hospital. You were very badly injured. Here's the doctor now.'

There were hurried footsteps, then the swishing of metal curtain rings and Dr Jefford leaned over her. She felt his fingers around her wrist. She tried to snatch it away.

'I'm just taking your pulse, Iris, no need to worry. You've had a dreadful shock.'

Dreadful shock? Whatever could he mean?

She caught sight of Sister standing behind him, an anxious frown on her face.

'How long have I been asleep?'

'On and off for a couple of weeks. We had to operate to remove the bullet,' the doctor replied gently.

'Bullet?' she asked, confused, and then it came back to her gradually, like pieces of a jigsaw. The Japanese plane bursting into view, the ack-ack of the machine gun, Nigel throwing himself on top of her, then darkness.

'Where's Nigel?' she asked. Her mother and Dr Jefford exchanged worried looks.

'He's not too good,' Dr Jefford said. 'We'll talk about him later. You just need to focus on yourself and on getting better.'

'I need to get up. Doc Bourne needs me up in the camp.'

She tried to sit up but the stab of pain in her shoulder made her gasp and fall back instantly.

'Doctor Bourne is managing just fine,' said Dr Jefford in a soothing tone. 'He has some new volunteers to help him up there. You're not to worry.'

'Can I go home?' she asked, looking at her mother, whose face she now realised was stained with tears. Her mother shook her head.

'Not for a while,' said Dr Jefford. 'We need to stabilise you first. You need to rest. I'll leave you with your mother for a few minutes, then we must give you some peace and quiet.'

He and Sister disappeared through the curtain and Iris was left alone with her mother.

'You gave me such a fright, darling. I've been here day and night, waiting for you to wake up. And now you have, I'm so relieved... and overjoyed, of course.'

'What about Daddy?'

Her mother's eyes flicked away from hers. 'Oh, he's been here too. It's just he's been called away on some urgent business by the maharajah. I'm going to go home now and will get the good news to him at the palace.'

'Ask him to come and see me, won't you?'

'Of course. Of course I will. Now, I must go, and you must get some rest.' Delphine stood up.

'I'm sick of resting.'

'But it's what you need, darling.'

'What happened to Nigel, Mummy? Is he here in the hospital too? I'd like to see him.'

Colour rose in her mother's cheeks and she dropped her gaze again.

'No... no, darling. He's not here I'm afraid.' She looked around briefly, as if to seek help, but then sighed and leaned forward. 'I don't see why you shouldn't know the truth. Nigel didn't make it. He was killed outright by the machine-gun fire.'

The shock was intense and hit her like a physical blow. Black spots began to obscure her vision again, then they were multiplying rapidly and soon she could see nothing but black. She fell back on the pillow, unconscious.

When she awoke, her mother had gone and Sister was standing beside her bed. Iris recalled that something dreadful had happened. At first, she couldn't remember what it was, just that there was a heavy weight of sadness pressing down on her chest. Then she remembered about Nigel and tears filled her eyes. Sister took her hand. 'Now, now, child. You mustn't upset yourself. You need to rest otherwise you won't get better.'

'How long will I need to be in here, Sister?'

'We don't know yet. You had a deep wound. It pierced your lung from the rear. It will take time.'

Iris stayed in the city hospital for another ten days. The routine was monotonous. She was awoken early for breakfast, the doctor would come and examine her mid-morning, lunch was served at noon. That was followed by visiting time, then an early supper and lights out at nine o'clock. Her father came to see her on the day she woke up. His eyes were troubled, and he seemed distracted.

At first, she thought it must be caused by anxiety about her, but after a while she realised that there was something else on his mind.

'What's the matter, Daddy?' she eventually asked. 'You look worried.'

'Oh... oh, nothing really. Just a bit of trouble at the palace.'

'What sort of trouble?'

'Well...' he was clearly wondering what to tell her and

when he eventually spoke, she could tell that he wasn't telling her the whole truth. 'There are riots going on all over the state. Part of it is about taxes, the usual thing of course, but the other part is that people are objecting to their boys being conscripted into the Indian Army to fight for the British. My feeling is that Congress and the Quit India campaign are behind the uprisings. The maharajah's having trouble containing it this time.'

'Oh dear, poor old you, having to deal with all that,' she said, but it didn't sound much worse than other issues he had had to cope with over the years: famines, demonstrations, floods, uprisings.

'It'll sort itself out eventually, I suppose,' he muttered. 'HH is beside himself of course.'

After he'd left, the monsoon broke. Rain lashed the windows of the ward and nurses went round with window poles, opening the tall sash windows to let in some welcome fresh air. It had been building up for days and Iris realised then how clammy and stale the air in the ward had got. She thought about the soldiers up at the front at Kohima. The battlefield was already a sea of mud, now the trenches, the roads and camps would be swamped too, adding to their misery.

The next day Sharmila came to visit her; she was sitting beside the bed when Iris awoke from a morning nap. Sharmila's eyes looked as troubled as her father's had.

'Sharmila! Thank you for coming to see me. How did you know I was here?'

'One of the Indian nurses on the ward is a friend of mine. She came to tell me.'

'That was thoughtful of her,' Iris said but at the same time thought how sad it was that her own parents hadn't seen fit to tell Sharmila that she was in hospital. It underlined their differences and how their friendship wasn't wholly approved of.

'But how are you Iris? You look very pale.'

'I'm getting better every day. I'll soon be out of here,' she said, making light of her pain and weakness. 'And how are you, Sharmila?'

'So-so,' she said forcing a smile. 'Things are just the same, actually.'

'Oh, Sharmila. I'm so sorry. Tell me all about it.'

'There isn't much to tell. Just that Deepak spends evenings away from home as he always did. I'm still convinced he's hiding something from me.'

'Have you tried talking to him?'

Sharmila shrugged. 'I've tried, but he always clams up. He won't talk about his past at all. In fact he won't talk about much at all. I wish I knew what it was all about.'

'Poor you,' said Iris, musing over the fact that she'd listened to her father's troubles only the day before. Perhaps that was the fate of an invalid, to listen to friends and families' problems, someone captive to unburden oneself to?

'And there's something else now too,' Sharmila said, brightening a little.

'Really? How mysterious. Do tell me.'

'I'm expecting a baby.'

'Oh, Sharmila. That's wonderful news! You must be overjoyed.'

'I would be, but for the situation with Deepak. I'm not sure it is right to bring a baby into the world when we are so unhappy.'

Then she dissolved into tears and although it hurt Iris to do so, Iris put out her arms to her friend. Sharmila came to her and they hugged until the tears subsided. When Sharmila had gone, Iris thought about her desperately sad situation and resolved to do what she could to help her friend.

It was the conversation with Sharmila that finally galvanised her to make sure she got better and was able to get out of hospital as soon as she could. Reflecting on Sharmila's visit made her realise that she'd changed so much since she set off for Imphal. At that point, losing Edward had affected her so badly, that she'd not cared what happened to her in the mountains, not cared if she lived or died. But during those weeks and months looking after the wounded, she'd seen so much death and suffering, suffered so much grief herself, that she realised now that life was a precious thing. She knew that she owed it to Nigel, who'd given his own life to save hers, to get better and to make sure that her own life mattered.

It was still raining on the day she left hospital. Her father's syce came in the official car to pick her up, Delphine in attendance. It was an effort to walk down the corridor and out of the front door, she'd only managed to walk across the ward a couple of times before that, but when she got outside she lifted her face to the rain and took in a gulp of the clean fresh air.

'Come on under the umbrella,' her mother said, waving it above her head. 'You'll catch your death.'

'No, I won't, Mummy,' she laughed and lowered herself gently into the back of the car.

The house felt cold and empty and, as she went through the front door and crossed the hall, it hit her that she'd been away a very long time. After a cup of tea, she went out onto the veranda to sit in one of the planter's chairs and to relax. It was wonderful to watch the rain on the lush garden, to feel the splash as it landed on the balustrade and to feel the cool breeze on her face. Her mother came to join her and sat down heavily in the chair beside her, flicking through a magazine.

'I think I'll go back to work at the hospital when I'm better,' she said. 'Sister told me that they still get wounded soldiers in every day.'

Her mother coloured a little, cleared her throat and put her magazine down.

'I'm afraid that might not be possible, darling.'

'I don't mean until I'm better. It will take a few weeks. I know that.'

'I was hoping not to have to break the news quite so soon,' her mother said awkwardly. 'But I'm afraid we're going to leave Nagabhari quite soon.'

'Leave Nagabhari?'

'I'm afraid so.'

'Where are we going?'

'Well, your father and I wanted to go back to England, but there are no ships at the moment. We'll have to wait until the war is over. Until then, your father has taken a job in Government House in New Delhi.'

Iris stared at her, open mouthed. She couldn't believe what she'd just heard. Her parents were committed India hands. She'd never heard any talk of returning to England before.

'But why? I thought you both loved it here.'

'Oh, your father says that Independence is just round the corner. It's only a matter of time before we'll have to go anyway.'

'But what's happened? Why now?'

'Your father has made his mind up. In fact, he's already resigned his post as Resident.'

Iris looked at her mother who looked away and began picking at invisible dust on her skirt. There was something odd about this she was sure. Her father had been Resident of Nagabhari for fifteen years and was set to stay until retirement. What could possibly have happened to change that?

15

Nagabhari, India, 1985

I ris got out of the rickshaw at the end of Church Road and stood looking down it at the old colonial bungalows and their overgrown gardens. She remembered how she used to cycle down this road to drop off dinner invitations for her mother. Every bungalow had been occupied by people who'd worked in the service of the Residency and she'd known everyone who'd lived in this street. Now, most were empty, and they were all derelict, roofs caving in, walls crumbling, windows boarded up. A few pi-dogs rummaged in a mound of rubbish in one driveway, and a group of children played on the steps of another bungalow. She walked along the potholed road towards the old church that stood amongst evergreen trees at the end, and remembered walking down here on Sundays with her parents to attend church services.

As she walked, she thought about Elspeth. Iris hadn't had the heart to challenge Elspeth about how she'd seen her walking nimbly up the side path of the hotel the previous evening. When Iris had gone into Elspeth's room, Elspeth had been sitting up in bed, with no suggestion that she'd been out of bed whilst Iris was out, let alone having gone for a brisk stroll.

'How was your *friend*?' Elspeth asked, emphasising "friend" sarcastically.

'Sharmila was in good health, thank you. The years have treated her well.'

'Well, that's good to know,' Elspeth's voice was resentful. 'After such a difficult start to her marriage.'

Iris took a deep breath, determined not to let Elspeth rile her. She didn't want to get into an argument, and she wasn't ready to confront her about the walking stick yet. She needed to think about it, to plan her approach.

This morning, Elspeth had been a little better. She'd managed to get to the dining room for some plain porridge and black coffee but had then gone straight back to her room.

'I think I'll sit down and let things settle for a bit,' she'd said. 'You never know. What are you going to do?'

'I think I might go and take a look at Church Road this morning. Sharmila told me that an old man lives down there who used to be the chowkidar at the palace. He often mentions my father, apparently. I'd like to go and talk to him about the old days.'

'Well, that *is* scraping the barrel rather. As I said, I'll just rest here for a couple of hours.'

Iris had been relieved to have the morning to herself and went straight over to one of the waiting rickshaws on the hotel drive and asked him to take her to Church Road.

She was nearing the church now and sure enough, there was an old man sitting in a battered looking chair in an over-grown driveway. He was reading a newspaper and as she got closer she noticed with surprise that it was the London Times. She stopped short when she saw the headline "Imphal Under

Seige", and realised that the newspaper must date from the 1940s. Everyone had steered clear of speaking about the war to Iris since she'd come back, but that headline took her back there, to that huge valley encircled by mountains. She still felt for the troops holed up there, at the mercy of the enemy, and those at Kohima too, trying to hold on to that bleak mountain top against all the odds.

The old man looked up as she stopped in front of him.

'Good morning,' she began, making a namaste with her hands and bowing her head. 'You might not remember me, but I used to live in Nagabhari in the 1940s. You used to work at the Lake Palace, didn't you? My name is Iris Walker.'

He put his paper down and beamed up at her, shading his eyes against the sun.

'Yes. I am Gokal, former chowkidar to the maharajah. And I do remember you. I do indeed. Your father, Mr David Walker was a very good man. He was an excellent Resident. The state suffered very much when he left. Please, memsahib, do sit down if you have time.'

He grandly gestured towards the end of a broken wall and she perched on it.

'Oh yes,' the old man went on. 'I often remember your father. He helped the maharajah in so many ways. He helped to solve all the crises in Ranipur state. But of course, a couple of years after he left we had Independence and the state was absorbed into India.'

He shook his head, as if that was a matter of great regret.

'And I remember your mother too. She was a great beauty. Often at the palace. We all used to admire her.'

'Well, she's still alive and she has many fond memories of India,' Iris replied.

'That is good to know,' the old man smiled, closing his eyes momentarily, remembering. When he opened them again, he said, 'I remember when you last came to dinner at the palace. It was when Prince Ranjit brought his friends from university in England. Do you remember that evening?'

'Oh yes. I've never forgotten it,' Iris said, her eyes faraway too, remembering that balcony under the stars.

'There was a young gentleman there. A Mr Stark. He was a very nice young man. I became quite friendly with his bearer while they stayed with us.'

Iris opened her eyes wide, amazed that the old man remembered Edward.

'I was very fond of Edward,' she said. 'We went on a few outings together before he left for the hills. I was hoping to see him when he came back, but I only got one letter from him. He didn't reply to my letters. I never heard from him again.'

The old man frowned deeply. 'That is strange. He seemed such a polite, well-mannered young man. I cannot imagine he wouldn't have replied if he'd received your letters.'

'I know. I thought the same. Perhaps he didn't get my letters at all. The post in the hills can't be very reliable. Anyway, I put it behind me in the end, but I still think about him, especially since I came back to India. I'd love to know where he went and why he didn't keep in touch.'

The old man was silent for a moment, then he said, 'His servant talked about where they were going. He swore me to secrecy. He said he wasn't supposed to tell, but one evening we drank some arak and his tongue was loosened. He talked more than he should.'

'Would you tell me? I would dearly love to know what became of Edward. At the time, I thought he had changed his mind about me. I could have asked Ranjit for news of his friend, but I had far too much pride.'

'I suppose at this distance in time, there is no harm in me telling you. I have kept the secret for more than forty years.'

'Please. It would really help me to know.'

The old man breathed a heavy sigh. 'Those men weren't just *friends* of Prince Ranjit's you know. They were on a special mission.'

'Special mission? What do you mean?' She stared at him. It sounded too fantastic to be true.

He nodded. 'The prince was helping them, providing them with funds, transport, accommodation. I don't know what they were doing exactly, or who they were working for, only I know there was more to their expedition than they told people.'

'What type of special mission?' she asked, her curiosity piqued. Could Edward really have been part of something secret? Her heart beat a little faster.

'I have no idea what they were up to,' the old man went on. 'But they must have been very brave men. As far as I understood, they were planning to go behind Japanese lines to work with the Nagas.'

'Was this part of a military operation do you know? Edward insisted they weren't going anywhere near the front.'

'All I know is that they were going to work with the Nagas on a secret mission. They were all expert in the Naga languages.'

'But that's amazing. Edward told me that they were going up there to set up schools. He specifically told me more than once that they wouldn't be going anywhere near the front.'

'They weren't allowed to tell anyone what they were doing. I should never have been told as much as I was.'

'Do you know where they went? I wrote to Edward at a village called Nangtek.'

'Ah, yes. Nangtek was on their route up the hills. But that village was only a stop off point. I did know the name of district they were bound for, but that is all.'

'It would be a great help if you could tell me.'

The old man scratched his head and closed his eyes for a long time. Iris shifted on the wall, the uneven bricks sharp through her trousers. He took so long to reply that she even wondered if he'd gone to sleep. But then his eyes snapped open.

'Ejeirong. That was it. Ejeirong district. I don't know which villages they were going to visit, but that was where they were headed.'

'Thank you,' she said. 'I will look it up on the map.'

As she left, the old man asked her to come back and tell him if she found out anything more about Edward's mission and she promised that she would. When she reached the end of Church Road she turned and waved. What a strange existence he led, sitting outside his derelict home, dreaming about the old days and chatting with any random stranger who happened to pass by. Then she thought about her mother in the nursing home, leafing through albums of faded photographs from their days in India. Was her life so very different from the old servant's?

The rickshaw-wallah was still waiting for her at the end of the road. He was asleep, lying back in the seat, his feet on the handlebars. She tapped him on the shoulder and he awoke instantly, then she climbed on board and he took off into the traffic. As they pedalled away, heading for the old town, Iris reflected on what the old man had told her about Edward. She could scarcely believe it, but thinking back, he had been very cagey when she'd tried to question him about his mission into the hills. And it was a surprise that the mission had military connections, but she'd also wondered at the time why a fit young man like Edward hadn't signed up for the army. He didn't seem the sort to have shied away from duty. Now she was beginning to get answers, or at least some of them.

16

Nagabhari, India, 1944

In those weeks after her return from hospital, the atmosphere between Iris' parents was more poisonous than ever. They barely spoke, and when they did, it was to snipe or complain about the other. They ate their meals separately and slept in different rooms. Iris didn't bother to ask what the issue was; they had gone through such phases many times before, but this time things seemed particularly bitter. She wondered vaguely if it was somehow connected with the decision to leave Nagabhari. Certainly, her father seemed withdrawn and preoccupied. It troubled her to see him like that. They had once been so close, but now he seemed to be putting distance between them.

One day she decided to tackle him in his study as he worked late.

'Are you alright, Daddy?' she asked, standing in the doorway. 'I just came to say goodnight.'

'Of course, darling,' he said, glancing at his watch. 'You

should have gone to bed hours ago. The doctors said you should take it easy.'

'I can't spend all my time in bed. I feel better up and about. I want to get back to normal as soon as I can.'

She went into the room and sat down in the leather chair opposite his desk. He looked up.

'You really should go to bed, Iris, dear. I need to get through these papers.'

She ignored his entreaty, which she knew was only a way of avoiding difficult questions.

'Why are we leaving Nagabhari, Daddy?' she asked. 'No one has given me a straight answer yet. I thought you loved your work here. I can't understand why you resigned.'

He looked at her for a second then back at his papers. 'It's time to move on, my dear. I've done what I can here. Independence is just round the corner anyway.'

'So, why not stay and help with the handover? Wouldn't they benefit from someone with your experience?'

He sighed and put his face in his hands. When he lifted them away his face looked drained and his eyes looked suddenly defeated. 'I'm sure they would, but the decision is made, my love. There's nothing more to say about it.'

'But Daddy. You've poured your life and soul into this job for years. Surely now is the worst time to leave?'

'They need a younger man to pilot them through these tricky waters,' he said evasively.

'What does the maharajah say about it?'

'He's in too much of a panic to have a clear view I'm afraid. What with everything that's going on.'

'Can't you change your mind? I don't want to leave Nagabhari. It's my home.'

'Look, Iris,' she sensed he was becoming impatient now. 'The decision is made and there's nothing you can say or do to change things. We'll be leaving for Delhi in ten days' time. Now, if you don't mind, I really need to get on with these papers if I'm going to get any sleep at all tonight.'

The next day, Iris decided she had to break the news to Sharmila. She'd been to see her a few times since she'd been back from hospital and each time she had come away more worried about Sharmila's state of mind than before. Sharmila had lost weight recently, her face looked gaunt and had lost its youthful vitality. Iris had been putting off breaking the news to her, but now the move was imminent, she realised she must tell Sharmila they were leaving Nagabhari before she heard it from someone else.

When she went downstairs in the morning, she was surprised to see a pile of wooden crates stacked in the hallway, and as she went out through the front door, she saw a truck drawing up in the drive.

'What's that truck, Viraj?' she asked the bearer who was standing by the front door.

'Removal lorry, memsahib. Come to take furniture to the station for Delhi goods train.'

'Oh no,' she said, dismayed, then noticed the sadness in the old servant's eyes. He had worked for the family for many years and when they left, he would probably be unable to find another job.

She took a rickshaw to Sharmila's house. Since her injury, it was too painful and she lacked the energy to cycle herself, and it was too far to walk. When she drew up outside Sharmila's drive, she noticed with surprise that the curtains were closed. The bearer looked relieved to see her when he answered the door.

'Where is Mrs Lal?' she asked and he shook his head despairingly.

'She won't come out of her room. She stays in her bed all

day and she won't eat anything. This has been the same for three days now.'

'Is she ill?'

He shook his head. 'No, memsahib. Not ill. Just... well, just sad. Perhaps she will speak to you.'

The bearer led her to Sharmila's bedroom door, a worried look on his face.

She knocked on the door.

'What do you want?' Sharmila's voice was weary. 'I've told you I don't want any breakfast and I don't want to be disturbed. Now can you just leave me alone, please?'

'Sharmila, it's me, Iris.'

'Oh, Iris! I'm not well. I can't see anyone today.'

Iris exchanged looks with the bearer. 'What's wrong with you?'

'You know. Morning sickness. With the baby.'

'Let me in, Sharmila. Please, I need to talk to you.'

'What about?'

'It's important. I need to see you about something.'

'Can't you tell me from out there?'

'No. I need to speak to you properly.'

There was a long pause and Iris could hear shuffling footsteps in the room. Finally came the sound of the key in the lock and the door was opened a fraction. The room was dark, and a sickly smell wafted out.

'Come on in then,' Sharmila said reluctantly pulling the door open.

Iris thanked the bearer and stepped inside.

'Can I open the curtains?' Iris asked, striding to the window and pulling them aside. Light flooded in. She opened the window too and switched on the ceiling fan.

'You might feel better if you got dressed,' she said.

'What difference would it make?' Sharmila hung her head. 'There's nothing to get dressed for.'

She wrapped her dressing gown around her more firmly, sat down at the dressing table and began to brush her long, dark hair.

'So, what did you want to see me about?' she asked, watching Iris in the mirror.

'I have some news.'

'It doesn't sound like good news.'

Iris shook her head. 'I'm afraid it's not. My father and mother have decided to leave Nagabhari. In fact they have decided to leave India altogether when the war is over. In the meantime we're going to live in Delhi.'

Sharmila dropped her hairbrush. In the mirror, Iris saw the shock in her eyes, and something else too. Was it fear?

'What will I do without you?' she said in a weak voice. Iris went to her and put her arms around Sharmila's shoulders, holding her tight.

'We can keep in touch. We can write as often as we want.'

'It won't be the same,' Sharmila whispered. Tears formed in her eyes and rolled down her cheeks.

'You have so much to look forward to,' Iris insisted. 'There's your baby to prepare for. You must be excited about that.'

'In a way. But I'm sure Deepak isn't. My pregnancy hasn't changed anything between us. If anything, he's even more distant than before.'

'Have you talked to him?'

'I've tried. The other day, I really pressed him to speak about his past, but he just went into his study and shut the door on me. He's hardly spoken to me since then.'

'I really wish there was something I could do to help, Sharmila.'

Over the course of the next two hours, Iris managed to persuade Sharmila to take a shower and get dressed. Then they went out onto the veranda together and the bearer brought them chicken curry and rice for lunch. By the time she left, in the middle of the afternoon, Sharmila was smiling. She stood on the front porch to wave Iris goodbye.

'I'll come and see you tomorrow,' Iris promised. 'But you must be up when I call!'

'I will be,' Sharmila replied. 'Oh, and Iris... thank you for everything.'

But as Iris walked away from the bungalow, she wondered if there was something more she could do to help Sharmila before she left Nagabhari. She was aware that once she'd gone it would be all too easy for Sharmila to slip back into despondency. She thought about it long and hard as she walked towards home, looking out for a rickshaw, and by the time one came into view and she flagged it down, she had formed a plan.

THE NEXT MORNING, Iris got up early and caught a rickshaw to the end of Sharmila's road, paid the rickshaw-wallah and walked the rest of the way. When she was almost at the bungalow, she waited in the road out of sight of the gate. The sun was already up and beating down and within a few minutes she was hot and perspiring. But at eight o'clock her efforts and patience were rewarded. She heard the front door slam, the sound of footsteps on the gravel and then Deepak appeared in the driveway, dressed in a suit, his leather book bag slung across his back. She let him walk a little way down the road towards the university, then she started following him. When he was a couple of hundred yards away from the bungalow, she hurried to catch up with him and tapped him on the shoulder.

'Deepak.'

He turned to look at her, surprise in his gentle, brown eyes.

'Iris? What are you doing here so early?'

'I want to talk to you. About Sharmila.'

'Sharmila?'

'Yes. I'm worried about her. She seems very unhappy.'

Deepak began to walk, his shoulders drooping. 'She is fine. It isn't your concern anyway.'

'But it *is* my concern, Deepak. She's my friend. And I'd like to help her if I can.'

'So how is it helping her to come to speak to me like this?'

'It's all I could think of. Please, Deepak, if you love her, which I know you do, you'll talk to me. I'm worried about her state of mind and I'm about to leave Nagabhari. I need to be sure she's going to be alright once I've gone.'

She watched his face anxiously, worried that he was going to get annoyed and tell her to stop interfering and leave him alone, but from his expression she could tell that he was thinking carefully about what she'd said. They walked along in silence until they reached the wrought iron gates of the English faculty.

'Look, I have to give a lecture now,' he said. 'But I could meet you at lunchtime. If you come back here at twelve o'clock, we could go for a walk and talk things through.'

'Alright,' she said, relieved. 'That sounds good. Thank you, Deepak.'

She watched him walk towards the building. A group of students came up to speak to him, and instantly he straightened up, his shoulders squared and he became animated. He walked inside the building with a spring in his step, laughing and chatting in the centre of the group. Iris reflected on the change in his body language as he entered the place where he must feel most at home.

She had nothing to do until noon, so she went up to the university library and whiled away the hours reading into the history and anthropology of the Naga people. She wanted to find out if there might be some sort of clue there as to the mission that Edward had embarked upon into the hills with his two companions. But there wasn't much information about the Nagas at all. There was a dusty old book by a Victorian anthropologist who had lived amongst the Naga people for years. She gleaned that there were many different ethnic groups within the tribe, and that they spoke a variety of languages and dialects. She read about their love for colourful art and design, their food, their customs and in particular their strong tradition of headhunting which was still alive and well in the 20th century, despite having been forbidden by the British. It made shivers run down her spine.

When she had read enough and needed a break, she remembered that when she'd entered, she'd seen the daily newspapers laid out in the reception area of the library. At home, her father had instructed the bearers to take the newspapers straight to him in his office, so she wouldn't be troubled by them, but now she couldn't resist looking at the headlines. *Japs worn down at Imphal* pronounced the Times of India. She seized the paper and read that Japanese attacks were being rebuffed daily by the allied forces and that it was clear that the enemy was running out of food and supplies. The 20th Indian Division of General Slim's 14th Army had beaten the Japanese away from Shenam ridge but the battle continued. She stared at the grainy photo of a muddy hilltop, where all vegetation had been blasted away apart from a few battered trees. Soldiers in tattered uniforms and holding guns, staggered through billowing clouds of smoke.

She was instantly back there in the camp, enemy planes screaming overhead, the constant sound of shelling in her ears, fountains of earth flying up all around her. She dropped the paper and her hands went automatically to cover her ears; she sat down heavily, sweating profusely. She remembered the weight of Nigel's body crushing hers, the horrific sight of his smashed skull. She sat there on the hard, wooden chair for a long time, taking deep breaths, trying to remain calm. And, as she gradually settled, she realised that perhaps her father was right not to let her see the headlines. She clearly had a long way to go to come to terms with Nigel's death and with what had happened to her up at Kohima.

It was almost twelve o'clock, so she made her way back through the university grounds to the entrance to the English faculty. She'd only waited a few minutes when Deepak came out of the building, alone this time, and crossed the drive towards her. He had that despairing look about him again, but when he caught sight of her, he smiled.

'Shall we go to the canteen and have a bite to eat, then take a walk around the grounds?' he suggested. 'We can find a quiet corner so we can talk. I have a free period after lunch so we can take our time.'

'Yes, that would be nice. I could do with a drink at least.'

So, they went back inside and queued with the students for curry and rice, collected a glass of water each and made their way to a table at the far corner of the refectory, away from the crowd.

'Thank you for agreeing to talk to me, Deepak,' Iris began. 'I wouldn't have asked, only I'm beside myself with worry about Sharmila.'

'I know. I know, and I'm sorry. I love her deeply, but there are things I can't speak to her about.'

'Is it about your time in Ganpur? Perhaps you could tell me instead?'

He hesitated, his fork halfway to his mouth. 'There are things about my past, things that happened in Ganpur, that I deeply regret and have never spoken about. I let the memories eat away at me. I suppose it's why I won't let Sharmila close.'

'You *should* talk about them, Deepak. It might help to get them off your chest.'

Again, he hesitated, and carried on eating. She could see from his eyes that he was debating with himself whether to tell her. Finally, when he'd finished his meal and dabbed his mouth on a napkin, he said,

'If I were to tell you, would you promise never to tell these things to another living soul?'

'Of course. You can trust me, Deepak. I'll be gone from Nagabhari anyway in a few days. Please tell me if it might help you and Sharmila to be close again.'

'Alright,' he said finally, pushing his plate away and getting up from his seat. 'Let's take a walk in the gardens.'

17

They strolled down a long avenue shaded by a row of eucalyptus trees. Deepak was silent for the first few minutes. He seemed to be working out where to begin. Finally, he started talking.

'When I went on an exchange programme from Benares University to Ganpur, I was very young and very naive. My parents weren't wealthy, my father was a silk merchant in Benares and struggled to make a good living. I went to the local government school and worked hard. I loved my studies and was quick to pick up the English language. One day, a local benefactor came to the school. My teachers picked a few of us to give readings to him. He liked my English pronunciation and offered to pay for me to stay on at school and take the entrance exams for Benares university.

'At first my father was reluctant to agree. He wanted me to leave school at the age of twelve and follow him into the family business, but my mother and teachers persuaded him to let me stay on and study. I used to work in his business in the evenings, balancing the books, preparing invoices. I worked hard at school and sat the university entrance exams when I was eighteen. I'm pleased to say I gained a scholarship for the university to study English literature and started the following year.

'My undergraduate years passed uneventfully enough and I gained a first-class degree. I went on to do postgraduate studies and began teaching undergraduates at the same time. In due course, I gained my doctorate. Life was good. I was happy, there in Benares at the university, but there were rumblings at home. My father had started talking about me getting married and he even had a suitable girl lined up for me; the daughter of a fellow merchant I'd known since childhood. Although I liked the girl, I didn't want that future for myself and didn't want to be tied down. I refused to go along with my father's plan. We argued about it again and again and eventually he cut me off financially and also from his business, even refusing to see me at all after that. My mother would come in secret to my university rooms to bring me food and clothes. The whole thing upset her very much and I could see the strain on her face each time she visited.

'So, when the opportunity came up to go on a teaching scholarship to Ganpur University, I was more than willing to apply. I persuaded my professor to give me a good reference and sure enough I got the place. I was so excited setting off on the train with my trunk and my books in a leather bag. Looking back now, I realise how young and naïve I was back then. Ganpur is over four hundred miles from Benares, and I was glad to be getting away from my father and all the unpleasantness that had marred the previous few years. My only regret was leaving my mother behind. She came to the station to see me off and I realised then that the rift between me and my father had aged her. Her face was thin and lined, even though she was not yet fifty years old. She stood on the platform, wringing her hands, tears running down her cheeks as the train drew out of the station. I was her only child, and it was hard for her to say goodbye, especially in those difficult circumstances. It was hard for me too, but I tried to put it behind me and look forward to my new life.

'Ganpur University was much smaller and less prestigious than Benares and at first I found that my new colleagues rather resented my presence, taking me for an arrogant inter-loper. They were worried that I had come in with new ideas intending to shake them up and tell them how to do things properly. Nothing could have been further from the truth. I was deeply shy and diffident, unsure of my abilities and certainly not about to try to lord it over my peers. But because of the way I was ignored, even shunned by them, I became withdrawn and unhappy within a few short weeks of arriving in Ganpur.'

'Poor you, Deepak,' said Iris, looking at him with sympathy. 'That sounds dreadfully lonely. And so disappointing too.'

'It was. Very disappointing. I had so looked forward to my new life. And added to that, my quarters were far from congenial. There was nowhere for me to stay on the campus, so I had to find my own lodgings in the town. I didn't have much money to spare, but I managed to rent a room in the old town, above a workmens' canteen on a busy street. The canteen stayed open into the small hours. It was where rickshaw-wallahs and taxi drivers went for a bite to eat after their late shifts. They were raucous and rowdy, so I got very little sleep and my work began to suffer. That gave my colleagues at the university another stick to beat me with, which in turn compounded my misery.

'But I still loved the work, and I got so much satisfaction from teaching students. The students in Ganpur needed far more help and support than those at Benares. They tended to come from less comfortable backgrounds, many of them having to take jobs alongside their studies, but that brought its own rewards. Even if the academic staff had no time for me, my students appreciated my efforts. They were the reason why I forced myself to stay and didn't go straight back to Benares, defeated, within the first few months.

'I gradually began to make friends in the old town too. When I couldn't sleep, instead of lying awake resenting the noise coming up through the floorboards from the canteen, I would get dressed and go down there and get a cup of chai and some soup and talk to the locals.

'That was where I first met men in the independence movement. Discontent was rife in the town amongst the lowliest workers. They were convinced that the reason for their low pay and poor conditions was British rule. A particular target for their anger was Reginald Holden, the District Officer of Ganpur. He was said to be very hard-line. He had suppressed previous demonstrations by sending armed police onto the streets, arresting the leaders and having them beaten up in prison. If anything, his approach hadn't crushed the local movement or even cowed it, it had made it stronger than ever. More and more previously peaceable men joined up, but it had driven the movement even further underground than before.

'When Holden passed a decree to raise property taxes in the town, the time came for a demonstration. The activists who gathered in the canteen poured all their time and energy into organising a march. I volunteered to go along, holding a placard, declaring "British Robbers Out". I didn't say anything to my professor or my colleagues at the university. I knew they would disapprove. I might even lose my job over it.

'I was a little nervous of being recognised as I set out on the march through the old town, bound for the business district and Government House where Holden had his office.

The atmosphere was electric, the energy and enthusiasm amongst the marchers was palpable. "British out" we all chanted in unison. The chanting was reaching fever pitch as we left the old town behind and entered Government Road, but it was then that the police pounced with batons. They'd been waiting in the arcades that ran along the fronts of the buildings, hiding behind the pillars, but now they swarmed in numbers, quickly overwhelming the marchers, pulling them to the ground, seizing their placards, beating them with batons if they resisted. Chaos reigned. Women and children were amongst the marchers, many of them were dashed to the ground, trampled by people trying to run away from the police. A policeman came for me. He grabbed my placard and threw it on the ground and stamped on it. Then he whacked me with his baton twice, once on my back and once round the head. I blacked out for a second, then managed to stagger into the shade of one of the buildings where I collapsed.

'When I got back to my lodgings and looked in the mirror, I had a huge bruise on my head and another across my back. I was seething with anger, that such a thing could have happened to a peaceful demonstration where no one meant any harm. I took a few days off work, saying I had a fever – it was impossible to hide the bruise on my head, and when I did go back I had to cover it with my fringe.

'On the day I returned to work, my professor called me in and told me that there was a reception at the English faculty that evening. He said that some dignitaries were attending including the District Officer. He made it quite clear that he expected me to attend and to be welcoming towards them. He reminded me that a large part of the university funding came from British coffers.

'I couldn't believe that I would have to meet and be polite to Reginald Holden, after the brutality I'd experienced at his hands. I wondered if it was some sort of test by the professor, but I had no choice. I dressed in my best suit and went to the reception as I'd been ordered. I was introduced to several British officials, including Reginald Holden himself. He couldn't have been more charming or polite. He was a tall, handsome man, with impressive whiskers and an imposing presence. He shook my hand. He seemed to know that I was from Benares. He joked about me finding Ganpur very dull indeed after such illustrious beginnings. I told him I didn't think Ganpur dull at all, and he raised his eyebrows and said that it had certainly been exciting recently. Then he said that he knew I taught English Literature and wondered if I'd ever considered teaching Hindi. It turned out that his wife had expressed an interest in learning the language and he didn't want her to go to one of the "babus" from the bazaar as he called them. He said he would pay me handsomely if I would take her on.

'I thought about it carefully. I had no desire to spend time with a no-doubt spoiled memsahib, likely to be as entitled and arrogant as her husband. But how could I refuse? And at the same time, I needed money. It might mean I could find some-where more congenial to live.

'So, reluctantly I agreed, and two days later I found myself taking a rickshaw to the Residence on Wellesley Drive in the British cantonment, an area of Ganpur I'd never set foot in before. The house was beautiful. Painted white it was spacious and elegant, with an impressive, pillared portico and set in huge gardens, but as the rickshaw trundled up the drive I felt very nervous and intimidated by the grandeur all around.

'I needn't have been. Elizabeth Holden met me on the front steps. She was with her little boy, Arthur, who looked at me shyly and ran away quickly when his mother told him to go and play.

'She held out her hand to me. She was beautiful. Slight and fair, with pale blue eyes that seemed to hold an infinite sadness in their depths. She asked me to call her Elizabeth, not Mrs Holden.

'We hit it off right from the start. She took me into the dining room, a huge, high-ceilinged room with a long, polished table and that's where we always had the lessons.

'Elizabeth learned the language very quickly. She had an ear for music, which made it easy for her to remember words and inflections. I went once a week on Tuesday afternoons and each time she made great strides. Sometimes Arthur would join us and sit quietly, colouring, beside his mother. He used to join in the lessons sometimes, prompting her and helping her out. Having been born in Ganpur and growing up amongst the local children, he already spoke fluent Hindi.

'There was not a hint of the memsahib about Elizabeth. She was natural and warm, kind and gentle with everyone around her, especially the servants. I couldn't imagine anyone more different to Reginald Holden and I wondered how they had met and why they had married. As the weeks wore on, I could tell she was unhappy and she began to hint as much to me, by the odd word, expression or gesture. She told me that she didn't enjoy going to the club, that she didn't like the crowd there and that that displeased her husband. One day, I saw bruises on her arm. She saw me looking at them but quickly pulled her sleeve down to cover them. I asked her what it was and she coloured and stared at the table. She wouldn't tell me.

'I began to fear for her safety, and I also realised I was growing far fonder of her than I should have done. I began to live for Tuesday afternoons when I could summon the rickshaw to take me to the Residence and spend an hour admiring her quiet beauty and enjoying her company.

'Then one day she suggested we should meet up later in the week with Arthur and go into the old town, perhaps to the bazaar or the market. She said it would be a good way to learn and practice her language skills.

'I readily agreed, and we met on the Thursday. The three of us visited the bazaar in the old town where Elizabeth bargained skilfully for fruit and vegetables, then we went down to dhobi ghat on the river. We bought ice creams and sat by the water's edge watching the dhobi wallahs beating the washing on the rocks, and enjoying the sunshine. I remember that she asked me if I ever wished I could run away. I said I was happy with my life, and that I had no desire to do that and she looked at me with an odd, pleading expression in her eyes.

'It became a regular Thursday afternoon outing. We would meet somewhere in the old town, visit a temple, the market or just walk beside the river. Arthur seemed to enjoy these occasions, being able to run about freely, get dirty and eat what he wanted.

'She told me once that Reginald was very strict with Arthur and that he wanted to send him away to school. She said she was trying to persuade him against it as she thought it would be cruel. She told me that Arthur's health was very delicate.

'One day, she arrived at our meeting place without Arthur and told me that the boy was a bit off colour and was staying at home with his ayah. She said she had something to show me and took me through a maze of backstreets near the station and we eventually came to a lockup garage. She threw open the doors and inside was a shiny green sports car.

'Her eyes were brimming over with pleasure. She told me that she'd bought it herself with money her father had given her when she got married. She said that she used the car when she needed to get away and not be Mrs Elizabeth Holden for a while.

'I asked her if her husband knew about it and she said that she didn't want him to find out, but that Amir, the syce, and Ayah knew. She said they could be trusted to keep her secret.

'We took the car out and she drove us out of Ganpur and headed towards the hills. She drove fast, the wind in her hair, then she turned off the road and drove up to a lake in the mountains. She pulled the car off the road beside the lake.

'There, she told me that she had something else to show me and she pulled up her sleeves and showed me bruises on her arms, and marks around her neck. I was appalled.

'She told me that Reginald had hurt her during an argument about Arthur. Then she dissolved into tears. I took her in my arms and held her close and she lifted her face to mine and kissed me on the lips.

'After that we became lovers. She would come to my rooms above the canteen and we would make love in the heat of the afternoon. She would often cry afterwards and say I was her refuge and the only thing keeping her going. All the time I carried on going to the house to give her lessons and meeting on Thursdays to go to the bazaar with Arthur.'

Deepak paused and stopped walking. 'This may sound very wrong to you, Iris. But you did ask me to tell you everything and I'm trying to be honest with you.'

Iris looked into his eyes, deeply affected by his story. 'I'm not judging you, Deepak. I understand that you fell in love with Elizabeth and that she needed your help. Please, go on. Tell me what happened.'

They were nearing the boundary of the university gardens, and in one corner there was the ruin of an old building. Rumour had it that it had been a zenana house where the women in purdah lived before it was abandoned and the royal family transferred to the Lake Palace.

'Let's go and sit down in the shade of that old building,' Deepak said. 'The sun is very hot at the moment. And then I will tell you the rest of my story and you will see why it haunts me day and night.'

18

Nagabhari, India, 1944

Iris and Deepak made their way across a patch of rough ground on the edge of the gardens, past a pond choked with lilies, to the tumbledown building. They found an old stone bench in the shade to sit on. Iris reflected that this was probably where the women of the zenana must once have sat, to relax, and to look out at the pond and over the gardens. When they had settled on the bench, Deepak began to speak once again.

'Elizabeth and I carried on meeting for a year or so until things came to a head. She would often drive us out of Ganpur in her little sports car. We would head towards the hills and end up beside the lake she'd taken me to on that first day. There was an old, abandoned pavilion there where waterbirds roosted. It must once have been a bathing platform. There was something deeply forlorn about that elaborate old structure from a previous era that gave the whole valley an air of sadness. The very atmosphere of the place seemed to emphasise our own tragic predicament.

'During those months we fell more and more deeply in love. I thought about her night and day, trying to figure out a way that we could be together properly, but we both knew that if we ran away, we would be shunned by both communities, quite apart from the physical danger she would be in if she tried to leave Reginald.

'Often, when she came to see me, she had bruises on her back, her arms or even her face. We both felt powerless to do anything about it. Reginald had an iron grip on Ganpur and controlled everyone and everything in the city. She knew he controlled the police department too, so telling them about the way he treated her was not an option. She was most worried about Arthur, though. Reginald bullied and belittled the boy, and made his life a misery. Arthur grew weaker and weaker and became prone to bouts of sickness and fever.

'Then one afternoon Elizabeth came to my rooms and gave me some extraordinary news that was both fabulous and troubling at the same time. She told me that she was expecting a baby and that she'd been to see Giles Harris, the doctor at the mission hospital, to have it confirmed. She told me she had no doubt at all that it was my baby. When it was born that would obviously become apparent and she would be in danger.

'That galvanised us into action. We had to do something quickly. We planned to escape together and to take Arthur with us. I made discreet inquiries amongst friends and found a little house to rent in the hills behind Darjeeling. It was where some of the leaders of the movement used to hide out. It was miles from anywhere so we would have privacy, and also a very long way from Ganpur so it would be difficult for Reginald to track us down. I gave her a photograph of myself as a keepsake, telling her of my love for her and how happy I was that we would soon be making a life together at last.

'We planned to leave on a certain date, but then she came to me and told me that Reginald was insisting on her going away on a shikar with him into the jungle to shoot tigers. She said she had to go and couldn't think of an excuse. She promised me that it was only a couple of days and when she came back we would leave together.

'I pleaded with her not to go, to bring our escape forward instead, but she insisted. Something troubled me about the shikar. But even after everything that had happened, Reginald had her under his power. We said goodbye in the knowledge that we would soon be together permanently, and I waited feverishly for her return.

'On the day she was due back, I packed my bags and went down to the lockup garage as we'd agreed, but when I got there, Amir was waiting for me. Elizabeth must have told him that we were planning to leave together. As soon as I saw the expression on his face, I knew he had some terrible news.

'He told me that Elizabeth wouldn't be coming. Tears were streaming down his face. He said that she'd been mauled on the shikar by a tiger, and that she'd died of her injuries.

'I was devastated. I went back to my lodgings and cried like a baby. I didn't go into the university for over a fortnight – I had planned to write and tell them I wouldn't be coming back once we were away from Ganpur. I just lay in my darkened room letting grief take over. And as I grieved, I thought more and more about the circumstances of Elizabeth's death. She was on the shoot with Reginald. There was no one else there. How could it have happened that she'd been mauled by a tiger? Wasn't he there to protect her? I began to think that he must have had something to do with her death. Perhaps he had found out about her pregnancy and about us planning to run away together. The more I thought about it, the more I was convinced of his part in it. I became obsessed with the idea.

'Elizabeth's funeral was held a few days after her death. I couldn't go anywhere near the British church where it was to be held. I couldn't bear to see Reginald Holden in all his hypocrisy presiding over the funeral. Instead, I went to the temple and lit candles and laid offerings and prayed for her. When the funeral was over and I was sure all the mourners would have departed, I took flowers to the churchyard and laid them on her grave. I knelt there on the bare earth and wept for her and for the loss of our baby.

'When I went back to the university a fortnight later, my professor called me in. He looked embarrassed. He told me that my tenure there had come to an end earlier than planned. He said I'd been called back to my post at Benares.

'I was shocked. I asked him why. He told me that someone with great influence in the community had brought pressure to bear on the faculty. I didn't need to hear the name to know it was Reginald Holden. That was all the proof I needed that he had found out about me and Elizabeth and that it was he who had brought about her death.

'So, I went back to Benares under a cloud and although nobody knew exactly why I had been sent back before the end of my secondment, rumours swirled around me wherever I went; rumours about drinking, about incompetence, about affairs with students. Someone had made sure that my reputation was tarnished and that I would find it hard to keep my post without a fight. I knew that someone was Reginald Holden.

'Months and years went by and things settled down a little. I threw myself back into my career and tried to put Elizabeth and everything that had happened in Ganpur behind me. But no matter how hard I tried, I just couldn't let it rest. I was seething with anger and I let that anger colour everything I did. I became more and more anti-British and I joined the independence movement in Benares. I went on marches and protests and when the leaders saw how committed I was, they asked me to do more; once, I joined a mob who threw stones at government buildings in Benares, another time we sabotaged trainlines when a British dignitary was visiting the city. I was happy to do those things to help the cause that was so dear to my heart. It helped me forget the bitterness and sadness that was consuming me.

'During the holidays, I used to go back to Ganpur. I still had a fascination for the place where I'd met and fallen in love with Elizabeth, and I was still in touch with the men from the movement there. I would stay in a cheap guest house in the old town and frequent the canteen below my old rooms and some of the drinking dens in the backstreets. Although some protesters had been imprisoned, some even driven to suicide by Holden's treatment of them, the movement was still very much alive in Ganpur. Riots and marches were ruthlessly suppressed by the police under the direction of Holden, but that made the protesters all the more radical, all the more determined not to be crushed out of existence. In due course, I heard a rumour that Reginald had remarried. I felt deeply sorry for his young wife, whom I caught a glimpse of riding beside him in a limousine once. Like Elizabeth, she was beautiful, but she was dark and striking, not blonde and petite like her predecessor. They couldn't have been more different in looks.

'Then, one day, early in 1940 something happened to change everything. I had been asked back to Ganpur to take part in a protest. It was known that Reginald Holden was going to be participating in some sort of parade; a celebration of British rule. The leaders were incensed that he could be doing such a thing and were convinced it was being put on as an insult to them. So, a protest was organised to march in the streets alongside the parade.

'At first it was peaceful. The atmosphere amongst the protesters was jovial, almost like a carnival. Various floats went past bearing brass bands, dancers, displays of British engineering and business prowess, then Reginald's limousine came into view bringing up the rear. As it drew parallel with us, someone picked up a stone and threw it at the car window which smashed. The driver stopped the car. Instantly, someone wrenched open the back door and pulled Reginald out. In that moment I saw his face; his eyes were like those of a trapped animal. He knew he'd met his match.

'Then the mob set on him, kicking him, punching him. I was there egging them on at first, baying for his blood, although I wasn't close enough to join in. There was a piece of loose kerbstone near where I stood and on an impulse I picked it up and raised it above my head, ready to dash it down on him and finish him once and for all, when suddenly Elizabeth spoke to me, as clear as day. I heard her voice in my head telling me that it wasn't worth it, and that I would regret what I was about to do. She said that she had forgiven him and I should let him live. Stunned, I dropped the stone, pushed my way out of the crowd and ran away from the protest. I suddenly wanted no part in what was happening. Elizabeth was right, I would have regretted it, but to this day I live with what I might have done to him if she hadn't spoken to me. I cannot forgive myself and I cannot get it out of my head. That is what is torturing me, why I can't be a good husband to Sharmila, why I can't let the past rest.'

Deepak stopped speaking and buried his face in his hands. Iris was stunned. She struggled to find words to comfort him. In the end, she knew she had to say something.

'But you didn't kill him, you walked away. You did nothing wrong. Why do you carry on punishing yourself?'

He looked at her, his face ravaged with grief and shame. 'But it's what I *would* have done. If I hadn't heard her voice. I had the intention to kill Reginald and I would have done it. My life would have been over then. It *should* have been over.'

'What happened to Reginald?'

'He died. The next day in hospital. He died of his injuries. Some men were executed for his death, probably not the right ones. It didn't matter to the British. In some ways, I wish I'd been one of them.'

'Has it ever occurred to you that it was actually your own conscience speaking to you, not Elizabeth at all?'

'It was her. It was her voice.'

'Perhaps your conscience spoke to you in her voice. It came from inside *you*, Deepak, that voice telling you to stop. It was you, not Elizabeth. You must hold on to that.'

'You know I came to Nagabhari a couple of years after that. Wind of my part in the protests had got to my superiors at Benares and I was asked to leave the university there. It took me a long time to get another job. It was only through the kindness of Professor Ramesh, Sharmila's father, that I was appointed here.'

'And that's when you met Sharmila.'

'Yes. When I met Sharmila, it was as if a new chapter was opening for me. She was so good, so pure and I fell in love with her. But it was a gentle, solid sort of love. Not the passionate infatuation I had for Elizabeth. When we got married, I thought everything would be fine from then on, but soon the guilt kicked in and I began to think I wasn't worthy of her. That she would be better off without me. The more I tried to shake off the past, the more it haunted me. I can't get away from the thought that I am that man holding that kerbstone about to smash another man's skull. I can't let that go.'

His face was ravaged with pain as he looked at Iris.

'Why don't you speak to Sharmila about it?' she asked gently.

'I'm so ashamed. How can I tell her that I had an affair with a married woman, that I participated in violent protests, that I almost killed a man?'

'You've said what a good person Sharmila is. She is kind and forgiving and would understand, I'm sure. She loves you, but she is so hurt that you are keeping things from her. It is destroying her and it is destroying your marriage and it can't be helpful for the baby. It's the only solution, Deepak.'

Deepak bowed his head for a long time, then took a deep breath and sat up straight.

'You're probably right. I've known in my bones for a long time that I have to talk to her. It's the only thing to do and my only way out of this. I already feel better having got all this off my chest. Thank you for persuading me to talk about it, Iris. I will speak to Sharmila this evening.'

19

Nagabhari, India, 1985

The day after Iris' visit to the old chowkidar from the Lake Palace, Elspeth announced at breakfast that she was feeling much better. She ordered a full fry-up, and to Iris' astonishment, munched her way through bacon, eggs, sausages and all the trimmings in a matter of minutes.

'It's good to be able to eat again,' she said, wiping ketchup off her mouth with a napkin. 'Now, what are we going to do today? I feel I've been missing out on the sightseeing.'

'Not at all, Elspeth. I haven't done much sightseeing while you've been poorly. In fact, the only tourist attraction I've visited was the Lake Palace with you. Since then I've just been killing time.'

'Catching up with your Indian friends,' Elspeth said, correcting her. 'So, what is there to see? I don't think I ever got out and about in my youth. I spent most of my time right here, in the club, propping up the bar, or on the army cantonment, pushing papers in that ghastly office.'

Iris smiled at her, thinking how different they had been when they were young; how different they were now. In her own youth, she used to live for the days when she could ride out into the countryside, either by bike or on one of the ponies her father kept in the stables behind the house. She would spend her days exploring the surrounding plain in the shadow of the distant hills, following winding tracks that led to tiny villages where people would come out of their houses to offer her food and drinks, and put garlands of flowers round her neck, as they would any stranger. She loved nothing better than to ride back to Nagabhari at dusk, when the setting sun would cast a warm red glow over the parched land, and the smell of dung and evening fires hung on the air, and farmers tending their cattle would look up and wave as she passed. That was what India meant to her. Not drinking at the club bar or gossiping on the cantonment.

'What are you thinking about, Iris? Your eyes have gone all dreamy,' Elspeth asked.

'I was just thinking about the old days. How wonderful it was to grow up here.'

'Yes, it was a very privileged existence.'

Iris was about to open her mouth to say that wasn't what she meant, but decided against it. There would never be a meeting of minds with Elspeth so she might as well just let things lie. Instead, she said, 'Have you ever been to the caves in the Naga Hills? The ones with ancient paintings?'

Elspeth shook her head.

'Well, why don't we go there? They are very interesting. I'm sure the hotel could fix us up with a taxi and a guide.'

'Alright. But will I be able to get up to the caves with my bad leg?'

Iris shot an incredulous look at her and was about to say something about having seen Elspeth walking quite normally without a stick, but stopped herself just in time. Now wasn't the time to start an argument, not if she wanted to get out and see the caves that day.

'I'm sure it will be fine. I can help you,' she said. 'There are only a few steps on the way up and once you're inside the caves the ground is reasonably flat if I remember correctly.'

Elspeth was silent in the minibus that the hotel hired to take them out to the caves and Iris stared out of the window, remembering her last journey out this way with Edward. She tried to recapture that feeling of soaring joy she'd felt that evening, heading out into the countryside with him, the feeling that the whole world was at their feet, that they were at the beginning of something momentous. She thought again about what the chowkidar had said to her about Edward's mission, wondering how on earth she could find out more about it. If it was under the supervision of the army, there might be some records somewhere, perhaps at home in the National Archives, but on the other hand, maybe the matter was so sensitive that no records had ever been kept. The more she thought about it the more she wanted to find out. That itch that she'd started to scratch by speaking to the chowkidar the previous day would never go away until she found out the truth, or at least tried her best to find out what had happened to Edward up there in the Naga Hills. But what more could she do? Who could she speak to here in Nagabhari who might know more?

She looked at the driver and guide, sitting up front, chatting away in Hindi, then it came to her. Perhaps there was a way of getting up into the hills herself, so that she could talk to people in the villages, ask them if they'd seen or heard of Edward and his companions. There might be people still alive who had met them. People didn't move away from those villages and some were bound to remember the war. That was it. She would try to find a way.

The minibus started to climb into the hills now and the road switched back and forth around hairpin bends, the engine straining up the steep sections of road. Iris looked back at the dusty plain, the lake with its fairy tale palace shimmering in the heat haze, and remembered how Edward had driven this same road in that open-topped car into the sunset. The landscape had changed very little since that day. Its savage beauty was timeless.

They reached the point in the road where the path to the caves began. The driver pulled the minibus off onto a parking place. The path had been concreted over since Iris was last here, proper steps had been put in to help visitors get up to the caves.

The guide opened the back door and a blast of heat surged into the airconditioned interior.

'Ready ladies? Let me help you out.' He gallantly held out his hand to Iris who climbed out quickly, then turned back to help Elspeth. Elspeth made a great performance of climbing out, handing her stick to Iris, then getting the guide to ease her out with both hands. Iris watched, biting her tongue at the fuss Elspeth was making. How could she be such a hypocrite?

The drama continued as Elspeth insisted on Iris holding one arm and the guide the other as they walked at snail's pace along the path and up the steps towards the caves. The guide, a good-looking young man dressed in a tight shirt, fashionable jeans and sunglasses was politeness itself. To top it all, Elspeth kept apologising for being slow.

'I'm so sorry. It's just my leg you see. Quite useless it is. Been like that for years. Nothing I can do about it.'

Once they were in the caves, the guide switched on his torch and flashed it at the wall paintings and sculptures, describing the myths they depicted and what was known about them.

'The caves date from 200BC and the work in them took place between then and 650 AD,' he began, the beam from his torch sweeping around the first cave, displaying the fabulous images of many naked women kneeling to pray beside a lake, behind them a row of bejewelled elephants. They moved on through the caves, and the guide explained that the paintings depicted many scenes in the Buddha's life, as well as other traditional myths.

'It's beautiful,' Iris murmured, awestruck once again at the skill of the artists and the brilliance of the colours that had lasted over 1000 years. Elspeth hardly commented, but each time they moved between the caves, she insisted on both Iris and the guide taking her arm.

Finally, they reached the last cave and the guide shone his torch around the walls. Iris remembered how embarrassed she had been when she and Edward had entered this cave, and how he'd gone out of his way to put her at her ease. She looked again at the naked bodies, twisted in ecstasy, the huge phallus on display in the centre.

'Well, this is quite disgusting,' Elspeth burst out in an outraged voice. 'I'm surprised at you, young man for bringing us in here. Two mature ladies, old enough to be your grandmothers. Can we leave now, please?'

'Oh, Elspeth!' Iris said, dismayed, ashamed at the way she'd spoken to the guide who was only doing his job.

'Trust you to stand up for him,' Elspeth said. 'I know where your loyalties lie.'

'Oh, Elspeth, *please*.'

'Come on. We're leaving. Give me a hand to get out of here.'

They walked back through the caves in silence, Elspeth

huffing and puffing with the effort, Iris too embarrassed to speak, the guide clearly hurt and offended. When they got out into the sunlight, Elspeth said,

'Now take us straight back to the hotel will you, young man? We've no need of your services anymore.'

'Elspeth!' Iris muttered again, appalled afresh at her rudeness.

The journey back to the hotel was also passed in stony silence, and as Iris stared out at the unfolding landscape, she felt resentment rising inside her that Elspeth had selfishly spoiled an otherwise pleasurable outing. The miles dragged and the journey seemed to take a lot longer on the way back.

When they finally arrived at the hotel, the guide came round to the side of the minibus and opened the door. He helped Elspeth out and she stomped off with her stick back towards the hotel entrance without a word. Iris got out, fumbled in her purse and handed him a large tip.

'I'm so sorry about my friend,' she said. 'She can be difficult, but she doesn't mean any harm.' Even as she said the words she wondered why she was defending Elspeth after her inexcusable behaviour.

'It's alright,' said the young man with a rueful smile taking the proffered rupees. 'Some people have difficult journeys in life.'

Iris smiled. 'You're right,' she said, brightening, 'What a nice way of putting it.'

He turned to go when she had a sudden, impulsive thought.

'Do you think it might be possible to go up into the hills?'

'The Naga Hills?' he turned back, frowning.

'Yes. I'd like to go up to the Naga villages. There is a particular district I have in mind. Ejeirong I think it's called. You see, a friend of mine went up there during the war and I never heard from him again. I'd like to go up there and find out whether anyone remembers him.'

The guide smiled. 'It is possible to go, but there are not many roads. You can only go so far by jeep, then you have to walk.'

'I can walk,' smiled Iris. 'I'm quite fit.'

'Your friend could not, though.'

'Well, she might not actually want to come. But what do you think, could you arrange something for me?'

He nodded. 'I know a guide who knows those hills well. He speaks the Naga language and could translate for you. He would be able to take you. You would have to camp, though, there is nowhere to stay up there.'

'Good. That sounds wonderful. How can I get in touch with him?'

'He doesn't have a telephone. I will go and see him this afternoon and ask him to come to your hotel tomorrow morning... alright?'

'Sounds perfect,' she said.

But as she watched the minibus drive away, it troubled her that Elspeth's behaviour would probably have coloured that young man's impression of tourists, of English women of a certain age in particular and she felt that it wasn't fair. She needed to have it out with Elspeth once and for all.

She went into the hotel and strode down the corridor to Elspeth's room. She entered without knocking. Elspeth was putting her kettle on. She looked round, startled.

'Elspeth! What was that all about?'

'What? What do you mean?'

'You were so rude to that poor guide. I was mortified.'

'Well, more fool you. He shouldn't have taken us to that filthy place. It was disgusting.'

Iris laughed. 'It is ancient art. The people who painted it

weren't ashamed of it. It's only in modern times we've got so prudish.'

'Well, hark at you. When did you become such an expert in ancient art?'

'I'm not an expert. I just think your behaviour was unacceptable. You should apologise to that young man.'

'I shall do nothing of the sort,' Elspeth said indignantly. 'Now, would you mind leaving me please? My leg is very painful. I need to rest.'

Iris couldn't help herself. She burst out laughing.

'Your leg? Your leg? Since you mention your leg, could you tell me exactly what is wrong with it?'

'It's nothing to do with you. But if you must know, it's an old injury from years back and I got thrombosis in it. It's never healed.'

Iris stared at her, wondering whether to deal the killer blow.

'Now Iris,' Elspeth went on, 'I know you want to defend that young man. You've always taken the Indians' side against your own people, but it's not on. There's no way I'm going to apologise to him. I've nothing to apologise for. Now, I really need to rest. So will you please leave the room.'

That was the final straw. Iris stepped forward, her mind made up.

'No, I will not leave.' She said it with such force that Elspeth flinched. 'I will not leave until you've told me why I saw you virtually running up the path at the side of the hotel and into the back door the other day when you were meant to be ill? Don't deny it. I saw you with my own eyes.'

'Running?' Elspeth said, her cheeks colouring. 'You must be mistaken.'

'I'm not mistaken and you know I'm not. You didn't need a

stick then. Your leg looked to be working perfectly well. You weren't even limping.'

'It must have been someone else,' Elspeth said in a thin voice and Iris could tell that she was weakening.

'It was *you* Elspeth. As you well know. Now can you tell me what it's all about?'

Elspeth sunk into one of the chairs. She looked deflated suddenly, but she didn't speak.

'Elspeth, please. Don't you think I deserve an explanation?'

There was another long silence, then finally Elspeth took a deep breath and began to speak.

'My leg *was* bad,' she said. 'Years ago, I hurt it when I fell off my bike. Oh yes, don't look so surprised. I used to ride a bike in those days, before I put on weight. It took a very long time to heal. As I said, it developed deep vein thrombosis so I had to go to the hospital for daily injections. I liked the attention. People were nice to me there. They were so kind that I didn't want it to get better. I wanted to be able to carry on going there, seeing the nurses. Well, it did get better eventually, and I had to stop going to the hospital, but that didn't mean that I couldn't pretend to have a bad leg everywhere else. So, I just carried on using my stick, limping a bit. People are so kind. They go out of their way to help. I don't want to be ignored.'

She stopped talking and closed her eyes and tears oozed out from between them and streamed down her plump cheeks. She didn't bother to wipe them away. Iris felt a rush of pity for her. What a very sad story.

She sat down opposite Elspeth. 'But why, Elspeth? Why did you feel you needed the attention?'

'My husband was a so and so. He was vile and abusive. He

never cared about me and he was never kind to me, not once the romance had worn off.'

'But you said...?'

'I said that he was a successful businessman, and he was for a time, but that wasn't the whole story. He got into gambling and lost all our money. We had to sell up, downsize. We did it more than once.'

Iris nodded. Things began to fall into place. The tight budget Elspeth was on, the fact that she was keen to save money and stay in modest guesthouses.

'I'm so sorry to hear that, Elspeth. But you don't need to pretend to have a bad leg, surely. People are kind anyway. People want to help.'

'Perhaps...' Elspeth said, dabbing her eyes.

'Well, why don't you try it, hey? While we're here in India? Abandon your stick and just see how people treat you. In my experience they are kindness itself.'

Elspeth looked at her sharply. A bitter expression on her face.

'Things always fall into place for you, though, don't they?'

'Whatever do you mean?'

'Well, you seem to have a charmed life as far as I can tell. Men falling over backwards to be with you...'

'I don't understand, Elspeth. I was married for thirty-five years. Since then I've never looked at another man.'

'I don't mean now, I mean back then.'

'Back then? But there was only Edward Stark...'

'Really?' harumphed Elspeth, then fell silent, picking at her skirt restlessly. Iris was left wondering what on earth she meant. But thinking of Edward, she remembered her plans to go into the hills and the request she'd made of the guide. While she was having such a difficult conversation with

Elspeth, she might as well warn her of what she was planning; things couldn't really get any worse between them.

'Elspeth, would you mind if I went away for a few days?'

Elspeth looked at her with a suspicious frown.

'Away? We're already away. What on earth do you mean?'

'Well, you know that Edward Stark went into the Naga Hills on a mission and he never returned? The chowkidar from the Lake Palace told me that it was a secret mission, with a military angle. They didn't go to set up schools at all.'

'Oh,' Elspeth said dismissively. 'I shouldn't take any notice of that charlatan.'

'He isn't a charlatan. He's an old man with no axe to grind. He just told me what he knew. He'd found it out from Edward's servant when they stayed at the palace.'

'When do you plan on going on this wild goose chase, then?'

'A guide who knows the hills is coming to talk to me tomorrow morning. I'll know more after that.'

'And how long would you be gone?'

'A few days. But Elspeth, why don't you come along? You can walk perfectly well. It would be great adventure. I'd welcome the company.'

That wasn't quite true, but she felt so sorry for Elspeth, given what she'd just told her about her life, and so guilty about leaving her alone here in Nagabhari that she felt honour bound to invite her.

'You must be joking. I've no desire to go up into those hills. Walking through the jungle? Camping? All those insects, and the heat! And the way those tribes live. I've never enjoyed roughing it at the best of times and I find India enough of a culture shock in itself. I don't know why you're going either, Iris. Not after all these years.'

'Well, I don't mind a bit of hardship if it means I might be able to find someone who remembers Edward. I've always wondered what happened to him. You see, I only had one letter from him after he'd gone, then he stopped writing.'

'Have you ever considered that he stopped writing because he didn't want to see you again?'

'Yes. I did wonder that. I tortured myself with that thought and I believed that was the reason for a long time. But there has always been a niggling doubt in my mind. And now I'm here, back in India, it's been troubling me a lot.'

'Well, to my mind it's your vanity at stake here. He stopped writing to you. He didn't want to see you again. Why can't you just accept it and get over it?'

'Perhaps you're right,' Iris mused. 'It might well be my vanity. But still, he was so sure he would come back to me. He made all sorts of promises. So, when he stopped writing it was a terrible shock.'

'Oh, he was just a typical man. They're all like that,' Elspeth said dismissively. 'I don't know why you thought he would be different.'

'He *was* different,' said Iris, thinking of Edward's earnest face, his gentle eyes looking into hers.

I'll come back for you, Iris.

'Clearly not,' Elspeth said tartly, then a new look entered her eyes. It was that cruel, mischievous look that she took on when she remembered something damning from the past or when she wanted to cause trouble.

'You know, it might have had something to do with your mother,' Elspeth said.

'My mother?' Iris stared at her, open-mouthed. Whatever did she mean? 'What would my mother have to do with it?'

'Well, it stands to reason.'

She thought of her mother embracing her when Edward

had gone and her soothing voice saying words that made no sense. *I know exactly how you feel, Iris.*

'Yes. Your mother. Don't you know? Don't tell me you don't know.'

What was this about? Iris recalled that Elspeth had dropped a few acerbic comments about Delphine during the trip. Iris hadn't taken much notice of them, but this was serious.

'Know? Know what?' she asked.

Elspeth laughed then, long and hard. A cruel, mocking laugh.

'Elspeth why are you laughing? No, I don't know. I don't know what the hell you're talking about.'

'Oh, for goodness' sake. Why are you pretending? Everyone knew. The whole community knew about it. You *must* have known.'

'Known what?'

'Well, all I can say is that Edward Stark probably found out about your mother and ran a mile from you to avoid a scandal. So, I really don't know why you're chasing after that young man forty years after he left you.'

Iris sat looking at Elspeth, whose eyes were full of vindictive satisfaction. She was stunned into silence.

20

India, 1944

In the half-light of the early morning, Iris stood on the platform at Nagabhari station with her parents, waiting for the six o'clock train. It would take them to Siliguri where they would change onto the night mail to New Delhi. The whole journey would take two days and two nights. Iris normally loved travelling across India by train; she loved the rituals of the railway, the colour and clamour of the stations and the feeling of travelling across a vast landscape. But this time she was dreading the journey. It would take her away from the place she loved.

It was a few minutes after dawn, and the sun had just risen behind the Naga Hills, staining the whole sky red and pink, shot through with streaks of gold. She felt a pang of sadness that this was probably the last time she would watch the sun rise over those distant hills. She thought of all the times she'd watched the sunrise while riding or cycling out for a day in the countryside.

Tears flooded her eyes at the realisation that they were

finally leaving the place where she'd spent so many happy years. She would never go out into the surrounding villages again, visit the overgrown temples, the caves, the hidden lakes, or hunt for bargains in the Nagabhari bazaar. She would never again go to the places where Edward had driven her, to savour those precious memories. It pained her too that she was leaving behind the place where she'd fallen in love and had felt more joy than she'd thought it possible to feel.

She glanced at her father. His shoulders drooped with sadness, but his jaw was set and he looked grimly determined. She knew he didn't want this any more than she did, but something he wasn't talking about had driven him to it. What, she hadn't been able to glean. Neither he, nor her mother had given away anything other than to say it was the right time to move on.

She was surprised at the lack of ceremony that had accompanied her father's leaving Nagabhari. After all, he had been Resident and Political Agent of Ranipur State for more than fifteen years. There had been a small reception at the club and he'd held a dinner for his closest colleagues at the Residence, but the family hadn't been invited to the palace for a farewell dinner. Perhaps the maharajah was bitter about losing his closest advisor? He was known to be mercurial and to harbour grudges, and maybe he felt snubbed. Iris didn't want to speculate, but she did know that she would miss going to the Lake Palace; the excitement of setting off across the lake in the maharajah's barge in the scented evening air, seeing the lights of the palace glittering from afar.

At last, the train puffed into the station and they were ushered aboard the first-class carriage by the guard. Iris' compartment was next to her parents'. Porters brought their luggage on board, stowing Iris' trunk under the window and her night case on the luggage rack. She tipped them generously and they left her alone in the compartment, pulling the sliding door shut. She sat on the bench seat and watched as the train pulled out of the station and began to gather speed through the outskirts of the town. Exposed to the track were dwellings that nobody wanted to acknowledge, especially not the British. It was a shanty town, where people lived by begging at the station. Their homes were beside the tracks under tarpaulins and in old railway carriages. Some slept out in the open under threadbare blankets. Skinny children, either naked or dressed in rags, played in the earth amongst the pi-dogs.

Every Indian town and city had such a community, but Iris couldn't help thinking that the recent famines in Ranipur State that the maharajah had been unable to prevent had been the cause here. She shook her head as they passed, thinking of the extravagant life most in the British community lived in comparison, as did the royal family over in their glittering palace, well away from the town and all its squalor.

The train pulled away from the town and Iris stared out at the familiar countryside, picking out landmarks. They passed the patch of jungle where the deserted temple nestled; the one she'd visited with Edward. She recalled with a pang how he'd kissed her there, leaning against the maharajah's car. She could still feel the touch of his body against hers all these months later. The train rattled on, passing a couple of small lakes where water birds waded and early morning fishermen cast their nets from little boats. Then the landscape began to look less familiar. It was greener here; they had moved away from the plain and were entering a great river valley.

There was a knock on the compartment door. 'Breakfast?' the steward hovered with a tray. She motioned him to come inside and put it down on the table.

As she sipped her coffee and munched through a large

breakfast of porridge, scrambled eggs, toast and fruit, she thought back over her last days in Nagabhari. She felt a lot happier at leaving Sharmila now. Things really seemed to have changed for her friend.

Two days after Iris' heart-to-heart with Deepak, she had gone to visit Sharmila. She'd felt a flutter of nerves as she walked down the road. How would Sharmila be? Would her advice to Deepak have made any difference? Would Sharmila know about her intervention and be angry with her? But as she approached the bungalow, her heart lifted when she noticed that the curtains were drawn back from the front windows. The bearer opened the door with a warm smile and as he showed her inside, Sharmila rushed towards her and enveloped her in her arms.

'I'm so pleased to see you, Iris.'

'You look a lot better. I'm so glad.'

'Let's go out onto the veranda. Kabir will bring our tea out there. I've so much to tell you.'

Iris smiled to herself and followed Sharmila out to the veranda at the rear of the house.

'Everything has changed between me and Deepak,' Sharmila said, beaming, seating herself at the table.

'Well, that's fantastic, Sharmila. What happened?'

'He told me everything. He said that he'd been bearing a great burden for a very long time and that he had to make things right between us before our baby was born.'

'That's such good news, Sharmila. I'm really happy for you,' Iris said, taking her friend's hand on the table.

Kabir brought the tray with the tea things and Sharmila paused while he set them on the table and she poured the tea.

'It was two days ago that Deepak came home from the university and said that we needed to talk. I was worried at first, I thought he was going to tell me that he was leaving me, things had been so bad between us. We sat down in the drawing room and he started to talk.'

She took a sip of her tea.

'He said that he had things in his past that he was deeply ashamed of, that he'd been hiding from me, but that hiding them from me had only made things worse. He said that he couldn't bear to shut me out any longer.'

'What did he tell you?' Iris decided that if Deepak hadn't told Sharmila that they had spoken, she wasn't going to reveal that fact herself. So, she needed to play along, pretend she knew nothing.

'He said that he'd been in love with a married British woman in Ganpur, that she had been expecting his child and they were planning to run away together. Then her husband, the District Officer of Ganpur, had taken her away on a tiger shoot and that she'd been killed by a tiger. Deepak was grief-stricken and joined the independence movement. Years later, he was there when a mob stoned the same District Officer to death. For some reason, he feels guilty about it, even though he didn't lift a finger to hurt the man.'

Sharmila stopped talking and looked at Iris with pleading eyes.

'Please don't judge him, Iris. I didn't. I was just pleased that he had finally told me what was troubling him all this time.'

'Of course I wouldn't judge him. That's an extraordinary and tragic story, Sharmila.'

'I know. I feel nothing but pity for Deepak now. I don't know why he kept it from me for so long. But now he's told me, I'm going to do my best to help him get over it. He deserves to be happy.'

'You both do.'

'You know, I think this marks a turning point for us.

Things are going to be so much better between us from now on.'

'That's wonderful, Sharmila. I was really worried about leaving Nagabhari. I didn't want to leave you the way things were. Did Deepak say what had made him speak to you about it?'

'He said that he'd spoken to a dear friend about it, and that the friend had pleaded with him to talk to me. He wouldn't say who the friend was, but I'm guessing that it was probably one of his fellow academics. There are a couple he's close to in his faculty. But he said he would never forget the friend's advice and he would be forever grateful to them. And I will too.'

Iris reached out and squeezed Sharmila's hand again, a lump in her throat. Her mind was at rest. It had been the right thing to do to persuade Deepak to tell Sharmila everything. Now she could leave Nagabhari secure in the knowledge that Sharmila and Deepak were going to be alright.

Now, Iris looked out at the great brown river the train was running alongside, so wide that it was impossible to see the other side, huge islands of lily pads floated on the surface, paddle steamers ploughed their course along the middle, too far away to make out any detail. This must be the great Brahmaputra that separated the North Eastern states from the rest of India. Crossing it marked a boundary. It would mean they were well away from Ranipur, moving into a different region altogether.

She thought about how she and Sharmila had exchanged addresses and promised to write. When they'd finally parted, they held each other and cried for a long time. It even made her feel tearful now looking back on it, but it comforted her to know that Sharmila and Deepak were reconciled.

The journey wore on. Iris passed it as she usually did; reading and watching the ever-changing landscape roll by.

Sometimes she thought she heard raised voices coming from her parents' compartment, and when she joined them for lunch they were not speaking to each other. Instead, they both addressed their remarks to her only. She could tell by her father's expression that he was boiling with anger. Her mother avoided her gaze and looked uncharacteristically flustered. The atmosphere was so unbearable that Iris went straight back to her compartment after the meal and didn't attempt to see them again until she was forced to at Siliguri Junction where they had to change trains. At the station there was some confusion about her mother's luggage and Delphine snapped at one of the porters. Her father apologised to the man and tipped him heavily.

On their way to the first-class waiting room to wait for the Delhi train, Iris' father bought a Times of India from the newsstand. He must have been feeling distracted because he made no attempt to hide it from her. So Iris sat opposite him and scanned the headline: "Siege of Imphal finally over; Historic meeting of 2nd British Division and Indian Division at milestone 107 on the Imphal to Kohima road." Her heart stood still and once again she was back there on that barren hilltop, the vegetation blasted away, only a couple of charred treetops remaining. She was chatting with Nigel, about to share a companionable cigarette with him.

This time she didn't begin to panic as she had in the university library. Now she was able to remember what happened next with a sort of cold detachment. It was as if she was watching from afar now as the Japanese Zero swooped in, spraying machine-gun fire, as she dived on the ground and felt the weight of Nigel on top of her. She realised, looking at that headline, that she had turned a corner in coming to terms with what had happened to her that day. She also realised that progress was being made by the Allied forces up there in the hills. Imphal was no longer under siege. That meant that there was no longer a threat of a Japanese invasion of India, and now, surely, the army was in a strong position to capture other places in Burma occupied by the Japanese.

THEIR NEW PLACE in the leafy suburbs of New Delhi didn't feel like home to Iris. Instead, it felt like a staging post on their route out of India. It was a beautiful house, befitting someone of David Walker's standing. But it felt impersonal. And after the small-town, parochial atmosphere of Nagabhari, Delhi felt impersonal too, like the great capital city it was.

Her father's job was at the palatial Government House, the beautiful sandstone and marble mansion designed by Lutyens as a statement of British power. Her father didn't talk about it much, but Iris gathered that it involved helping to prepare the ground for the British withdrawal from the sub-continent. Iris was proud that his last job in India was so important and influential. In contrast, her mother sunk into oblivion. All the life seemed to have gone out of her since they'd left Nagabhari. She spent her days alone on the veranda drinking spirits, rarely having visitors or going out. She made no new friends and never went to the club, which surprised Iris. Sometimes she didn't even bother to get dressed. When Iris' father came home in the evenings they barely communicated. Iris had given up trying to understand their relationship or why they remained together against all the odds.

At first, she tried to help her mother. She would sit with her on the veranda, trying to draw her out of her shell, to get her to talk about what was troubling her, but to no avail. Delphine clearly didn't want to be helped. She seemed to want to wallow in her own sadness. So, Iris filled the time by volunteering at the Delhi Military Hospital where soldiers with long-term conditions or with fever were sent. It took her away from the unhappiness at home, and she was glad to be caring for patients and making a contribution again, but she never felt that passion for the work or the camaraderie with her colleagues that she'd felt while nursing at the front.

She read the papers daily now and watched with interest as the Burma campaign gathered momentum. One by one familiar towns were retaken by allied troops; Myitkyina, Tamu, Tiddim; all fell to the British during the next few months. Then they were advancing in the Arakan, across the Chindwin and Irrawaddy rivers and alongside Chinese forces, up the Ledo Road into China.

As the months wore on, she carried on reading the news. In fact, on her way to the hospital each day she even bought her own copy of the Times of India so she could keep up with the campaign. Early in 1945, she read that the 14th Army had advanced through the plains of Upper Burma to Mandalay, which fell in March. They continued to advance south and retook Rangoon on 3rd May.

Iris went to the Regal Cinema in Connaught Place with another nurse after work one day to watch the elaborate victory parade through Rangoon staged by Lord Mountbatten. As she watched the flickering newsreel, all that flag waving and celebration, it took her back to those battles in the hills. She thought of all those young men, boys, some of them, who'd died up there so far from home, and all the wounded ones who'd recovered, their tearful faces when they thanked her before they'd left the hospital camp. How many of them had gone on to die for the cause? Was it really worth it? She left the cinema and went out into the steamy heat of the evening with a hollow feeling in her chest.

Although Europe was no longer at war the fighting in the

East dragged on over that long, hot summer. Finally, victory came on 15th August and the very next day Iris' father began to make preparations to leave India.

Two months later, she stood at the rail of the P&O liner that was to take them back to England. She stared out over the gleaming white buildings of the seafront at Bombay and the chaos and confusion on the docks, and her mind went back over the years she'd spent in India since her return from London. She thought of the people she'd met, the places she'd been and the things that had happened to her. Some of it seemed almost too extraordinary to be true. And as the ship set sail and drew away from the dock wall, setting out across Back Bay towards Elephanta Island and the ocean beyond, she looked back at the country she'd loved as it faded into a shimmering mist. While it gradually slipped away, all the memories she held dear began to resurface. She touched her garnet pendant, thinking of Edward, and to remind herself that it hadn't all been a fantastic mirage, that it had all really happened.

21

Nagabhari, India, 1985

The guide who greeted Iris in the lobby of the Lake View Hotel wasn't at all what she had expected. He was middle-aged and dressed in a combination of modern clothes and tribal costume. He had on a white t-shirt, over which he wore an elaborate necklace; rows and rows of fine red beads. Instead of trousers he wore a red and black sarong and topped off the outfit with brand new Nike trainers. He smiled broadly as she approached and put his hands together in a traditional greeting.

'I am Mengu,' he said. 'I live here in Nagabhari and some-times help people who wish to go up into the mountains. Your guide, Ali asked me to meet you here.'

'Yes, thank you so much for coming.'

They sat down together in the corner of the lobby and she explained her reason for wanting to travel up into the hills.

'I had a friend who went up into the villages during the war,' she said. 'I never heard from him again, so I would like to find out what happened to him there if I can. I recently found out that he was on some sort of secret mission to do with the military.'

Mengu rubbed his chin thoughtfully. 'Interesting,' he said. 'I know that there was quite a lot of collaboration between the British and the Naga people during the war. The Nagas didn't want to be ruled by the Japanese. But it might be difficult. It is a very long time ago. However, we can try. Do you know whereabouts in the hills your friend was going?'

She told him that he would have visited Nangtek and Ejeirong district.

'Ejeirong!' He laughed incredulously. 'Well, that is a very remote place indeed. Buried deep in the forests. Not even many Naga people will have gone there.'

He told her that they could take a Land Rover for part of the journey, but they would reach a point from which they would have to walk.

'There are jungle tracks, but no roads,' he said.

He explained that at night they would camp in the jungle. He would take two small tents and assured her that he would be able to carry most of their bedding and cooking equipment.

'Are you used to walking long distances?' he asked, eyeing her critically.

'I'm quite fit for my age and I love walking. I'm sure I'll find the hills a bit of a challenge though.'

'We can take our time,' he replied with a reassuring smile. 'There is no hurry.'

'How long do you think it will take to get up there?' she asked.

'Two or three days, perhaps. Maybe longer? It would definitely take longer in the monsoon, but we are lucky that now is dry season. In the wet it is very difficult. Leeches are a problem.'

'I remember,' she said wistfully, thinking of all those poor young soldiers plagued by leeches.

'Really?' surprise registered on his face. 'Have you been into these hills before?'

She nodded. 'During the war. I worked in a hospital camp just behind the front of the 14th Army. I went up as far as Kohima.'

'Kohima!' he said with reverence. He was clearly stunned by this revelation and from that point on looked at her with a new sort of respect.

When Mengu left, he gave her a list of items she would need on the trip. They agreed that he would come back to the hotel in two days' time at seven o' clock in the morning. He would be in a Land Rover with a driver and all the supplies they would need for a week-long trip into the hills. Iris paid him a deposit in worn rupee notes, which he tucked neatly inside his sarong.

As they parted, he said, 'You are a very brave lady, Mrs Grey. Very brave indeed. Not many elderly ladies would attempt such an expedition.'

'Hey! Less of the elderly,' she laughed as she waved goodbye from the hotel steps. 'See you on Monday.'

When she turned round to go back to her room, she saw with a start that Elspeth was standing in the hallway at the end of the corridor that led from their rooms. Just like before, when she'd caught Iris speaking on the phone to Sharmila, her face was clouded over with anger. She came forward, limping, leaning heavily on her stick. Iris wondered why she bothered with the pretence, now her secret was out.

'So, you're actually going on that fool's errand then, are you?' Elspeth asked sharply.

'It's just something I have to do,' Iris replied keeping her voice steady. 'I need to find out what happened to Edward up in those hills.'

'Do you think anyone will even remember him after all this time? He was just another Englishman passing through.'

'Well, not many Englishmen passed through those villages in 1944. Not that close to the fighting anyway. I need to find out more about his secret mission. Some of the older people might remember something about it.'

'I think you'll find that nothing happened to him up there. He went home and wanted to forget about you. It's a simple as that.'

'Maybe you're right. But if you are, I'd like to be completely sure.'

Elspeth stomped across the lobby to sit in the armchair that Mengu had just vacated. Her face was sagging with tiredness. 'Like I said before. He probably found out about the scandal.'

'Scandal? Elspeth, you must tell me what you mean. I know you wouldn't yesterday and we were both upset then. But now, please tell me. I really have no idea what you are talking about.'

'Ask the receptionist to get us some coffee and I'll tell you… If you actually don't know, that is,' she said sceptically.

Iris went to the desk and asked for coffee, then sat down opposite Elspeth. 'I swear that I really, really haven't the faintest idea what you're talking about.'

Elspeth drew a deep breath and said, 'Didn't you ever wonder why your father left Nagabhari so suddenly?'

'Of course. It was a huge shock to me to find out we were leaving. I was devastated. I didn't want to go at all, but Daddy was insistent. He said it was the right time to go and that Ranipur State needed a different pair of hands to guide them through Independence.'

'But he wasn't happy about it, was he?' Elspeth asked, narrowing her eyes.

Iris shook her head. 'He would never say so, but he was deeply unhappy about leaving. He loved Ranipur and he'd worked so hard for so long for the people of the state. That was why it was all so odd. And although he seemed reasonably happy and fulfilled in New Delhi, when we returned to England, he was a broken man. He could never get used to life there. I could tell that he was missing Ranipur and his old life.'

The bearer came with a tray and Iris paused while he put the silver coffee pot, jug, cups and saucers down carefully on the table between them.

'So, if you know the truth Elspeth, please tell me,' Iris pleaded, pouring coffee for them both.

'Everyone else at the club knew, so I'm amazed your parents managed to keep the truth from *you*.'

'The truth? Truth about what?'

Elspeth took her time, ladling sugar into her coffee, taking a sip of it, savouring it before replacing the cup on the saucer with a smack of her lips.

'Well, put it this way, if your father hadn't resigned, he would have been pushed. He did it in the nick of time.'

'But why? He was brilliant at his job. People said he was the best political agent Ranipur had ever had.'

'Because although he was a brilliant man, he hadn't made a brilliant choice for a wife I'm afraid to say.'

'My mother? What had she got to do with it? I admit she used to drink more than she should have done, but her drinking didn't get really bad until we moved to Delhi. That's when she really hit the bottle.'

'And did you ever wonder why?'

'I just thought she felt out of her depth there. She missed Ranipur, that's all.'

'Well, she had a particular reason for missing Ranipur. Did you not notice that she was particularly fond of going over to the palace?'

'We all loved going over there. It was a beautiful place. And you did too if I remember correctly. Where is this going, Elspeth?'

'Your mother had a particular fondness for the palace because she had a particular fondness for the maharajah himself...' She paused, a vindictive smile playing on her lips. Then she dealt the killer card. 'They were having an affair. Delphine and the maharajah. Had been for years.'

Elspeth's words hit Iris like a physical blow.

'An affair? My mother?' she stared at Elspeth open-mouthed. 'You *are* joking.' But even as she said it a few odd moments from the past floated back to her. Her mother's arms around her when Edward had gone away. *I know exactly how you feel.* The bitterness between her parents, and the way her mother had gone into a complete decline when they were in Delhi. It all began to fit together.

'Yes. She used to get a boat over in the daytime and meet him in the palace if the maharanee was away and your father was at the office. Didn't you ever wonder why she spent so much time out of the house?'

'I always thought she was out with your mother.'

'Sometimes. She used my mother as her alibi. And Mummy was good at keeping her secret. It all came to a head when the maharanee found out. She came home early once and... well let's just say there was an embarrassing scene and a big argument.'

'How do you know all this, Elspeth?'

'I used to eavesdrop on our mothers gossiping. Delphine didn't hold back on the salacious details, I can tell you.'

Iris frowned at her. She wished Elspeth wouldn't display

such obvious pleasure in imparting this embarrassing and distressing news.

'It put your father in a terrible position,' Elspeth went on. 'He could have divorced your mother, but he was far too honourable for that. He decided to stick by her. But then it became clear that if he did that, he wouldn't be able to keep his job. He had to choose. The maharajah was happy to hush things up and let him stay, but the maharanee wanted her pound of flesh.'

Iris recalled the maharanee. Her intelligent, all-seeing eyes, her stylish clothes, her luxuriant black hair. She was a feisty and persuasive woman, a woman who didn't suffer fools gladly. She was not to be crossed.

'You remember, she became a politician after Independence? Well even before that she was manoeuvring. She had friends in very high places; in Congress, in the Viceroy's palace, even in the British government. She had a word in the right ear and the next day your father was called by someone very high up in Government House. He was told to resign in no uncertain terms.'

'Poor, poor Daddy,' Iris said quietly. It all fitted now. The frosty atmosphere in the house, the arguments on the train, the slow death of her parents' marriage, first in Delhi and later on back in England. But still they stuck together. She wondered why he'd stayed. That decision had slowly led to his own destruction. She thought of him pottering about at their home in Tunbridge Wells, filling his time with gardening, reading, researching a history of British rule in India. Although he'd only been in his late fifties, he'd developed heart disease and died a few years after their return. It had seemed to Iris that he had no fight left in him, no energy, and no inclination to stay alive.

And she thought of her mother too. Alone in her care

home, fading fast but still beautiful in her own way. Delphine was now vague and forgetful; sometimes she didn't even remember Iris' name when she visited. But her long-term memory was sharper and fresher than ever before. She would talk for hours about India, with a faraway look in her eyes, remembering every detail of their home, the club, Nagabhari and the countryside around it, and various events they had attended. She would often sit with her old photograph albums, poring over black and white photographs of the old days, exclaiming in excitement as she turned the pages. Iris realised now that her mother rarely mentioned the maharajah. Perhaps she had trained herself so thoroughly to keep her own secrets that even though her mind was declining, she was able to guard them still.

Suddenly, she wanted to be alone. Away from Elspeth's triumphant glare. She gathered her things as calmly as she could and got up from the table. 'I think I'll go back to my room for a bit, Elspeth. I need a bit of time for all this to sink in.'

22

Nagabhari, India, 1985

I ris spent that afternoon and most of the next day making sure she had the right clothes and equipment for her trip into the hills. She avoided bumping into Elspeth, not wanting to revisit the painful discussion about her parents. As it was, it kept going round and round in her head. Little incidents kept returning to her that in retrospect made so much more sense now she knew the truth. She felt so sad for her father, whose career and life had been swept away by her mother's indiscretions. An image of his hunched shoulders as they waited on the station on the day they'd left Nagabhari kept returning to her. And the expression on his face. It was the face of a defeated man.

Instead of dwelling on these difficult memories though, she took a rickshaw to the covered bazaar and spent a couple of happy hours in the stifling interior hunting for bargains. Mengu's list told her that she needed walking boots, a good quality waterproof jacket and a walking stick. Making her way up and down the aisles amongst the noisy shoppers, she could have been that girl in her early twenties again, enjoying the opportunity to get away from home and from the confines of her own community to experience first-hand all the sights and sounds of India. At one point, feeling thirsty, she remembered there had been a chai stall in the far corner and shouldered her way towards it. It was still there! A middle-aged woman manned it now instead of the couple who used to run it in the forties. Iris asked for a cup of sweet chai and as she sipped the cloying liquid she chatted to the woman. It emerged that this lady was in fact the daughter of the couple who used to run the stall. From the depths of her memory, Iris recalled that a little girl used to sit behind the stall sometimes and the woman confirmed that it had been her. A warm feeling went through Iris thinking about how many links there still were with the old days; Sharmila, Gokal, this friendly stallholder. There were probably many, many more. It gave her a thread of hope that there would still be connections from the 1940s up in the Naga villages.

Fortified by the sugar rush from the chai, she pushed her way on through the bazaar. In the far corners she found stalls selling walking boots ridiculously cheaply and another that sold waterproof clothing. She made her purchases quickly, not even bothering to bargain, much to the bemusement of the stallholders. Outside on the street, she realised that before she went to the hills, she needed to pay another visit to Sharmila and also to see Gokal to let him know about her expedition. She dropped her purchases back at the hotel, asking the rickshaw-wallah to wait, and then set off again. There was no sound from Elspeth's room so Iris decided to let sleeping dogs lie and to simply creep out without disturbing her.

Gokal was sitting in exactly the same position in the chair in his front driveway that he had been when she last saw him. This time he was reading an Indian newspaper, though, instead of an English one. As she approached, he recognised her straight away.

'Miss Walker!' he said. 'How wonderful that you came back. Do you have any news for me about your friend?'

He gestured for her to sit down on the wall again. A sudden wave of shyness swept over her. Did Gokal know about the scandal surrounding her mother and the maharajah? From what Elspeth had said virtually everyone in Nagabhari knew about it apart from Iris herself. He *must* have known, surely; he actually worked at the palace. But then she recalled the respectful way he had spoken about both her father and her mother when she'd been here before. Perhaps he had no idea and Elspeth was exaggerating the reach of the gossip.

'I'm going up into the hills in a couple of days to see if I can find anyone who knew about Edward,' she said perching on the uneven wall. Gokal's mouth dropped open and he stared at her with astonished eyes.

'You know, after you left the other day,' he said, 'I remembered that I still had something that Edward Stark's servant left behind in his room. Stay here. I will go and fetch it.'

'Alright,' she said, intrigued, and waited in the heat of the sun while the old man bustled nimbly into his house. She stared after him into the gloomy interior. He was out again within minutes.

'Here it is...' he said and handed her a rusting metal object with a sharp pin attached to the back. 'One of the palace cleaners found it lodged between the floorboards after they'd left for their mission. It is broken, but it must have meant something to either the servant or to Mr Stark.'

'What on earth is this?' she asked peering at it. 'Do you think this belonged to Edward?' She felt chills running through her at the thought that Edward might once have held this object in his hands.

'It's some sort of pin or brooch,' the old man said, 'but it's broken. Look closely and you'll see. I try to clean it up sometimes, but the rust keeps coming back.'

She looked again and through the rust could just about make out two crossed swords, meeting in the middle. There was a blemish on each as if something had been snapped off, and along the bottom was a banner with the word "FORCE" inscribed along it.

'It looks like some sort of military badge,' she said. 'There's no indication of regiment or unit on it.'

'Take it with you, Miss Walker,' said Gokal. 'Show it to the villagers in the hills. It might help them remember, or they might know what it is.'

'Do you mind?' she asked, thinking how precious this memory of the past must be to the old man.

'Of course not. If it is of help, take it. But be sure to come back and tell me what you find up there.'

Sharmila was in her front garden pruning roses when Iris walked through the gate. She waved a gloved hand and came over to greet her with a kiss on both cheeks.

'How lovely to see you again! Come on inside, we can sit on the back veranda. Do you want tea? Coffee?'

They went through the house and the old bearer brought tea to the table on the veranda overlooking the garden.

'Gardening is a new hobby of mine,' Sharmila explained, smiling. 'Since Deepak died. I find it rewarding and relaxing too.'

'Oh, I love gardening too!' Iris enthused, thinking of her cottage garden in Surrey, overflowing with flowers and shrubs and how much pleasure she got from tending the roses just like Sharmila did.

'It's probably because we've reached that certain age,' Sharmila joked pouring the tea. Then she looked at Iris with serious eyes. 'Have you come to tell me you're leaving?'

'Sort of. I'm leaving for a few days on a trip into the hills.'

'The Naga Hills? Oh, Iris, you're not still hankering after that young man who went up there are you?'

Iris nodded. 'Edward? Yes, I'm afraid so. Since I've been back in India I've thought about him more and more. I don't think I'll be able to go home until I've found out what happened to him.'

'I understand,' Sharmila replied. 'It's terrible when something from the past just won't let you rest.'

Her eyes were on Iris' then. 'You're thinking about Deepak, aren't you?' Iris asked.

Sharmila nodded. 'You know I couldn't mention this in my letters before we lost touch, and I didn't feel ready to tell you the other day, but Deepak told me who the dear friend was who encouraged him to speak to me.'

'Oh,' Iris dropped her gaze and studied the curves on the elaborate wrought iron table.

'He told me shortly before he died. He'd been keeping it to himself for decades. I wish I'd known at the time because I've never had the opportunity to thank you. You saved my marriage and you made sure my daughter grew up with both parents in a loving family. I don't know what would have happened if you hadn't stepped in.'

'I was taking a risk,' Iris said. 'He could have told me to get lost, and it all might have backfired if you hadn't forgiven him. But I couldn't have left Nagabhari without trying something. And it was the only thing I could think of to do.'

'Well, you did the right thing. You were a true friend. *Are* a true friend.'

'We mustn't lose touch after this,' Iris said. 'I'm sure I'll be coming back to India again. I don't know how I managed to stay away so long. Now I'm back I realise how much it's in my blood, and how at home I feel here.'

'Perhaps we could go on a trip together, the two of us, sometime?' Sharmila asked.

'I'd love that. My current travelling companion and I haven't always seen eye to eye.'

Sharmila smiled conspiratorially. On her previous visit, Iris had told Sharmila a little about Elspeth and how little they had in common. 'You could always come up into the hills with me,' she said as an afterthought.

Sharmila laughed and shook her head. 'Oh no. I didn't mean anything half as energetic as that. I hate roughing it. Besides, I think that's the sort of trip you need to do alone. No, I was wondering if you'd like to go to Ganpur with me sometime?'

'Ganpur? Where Deepak used to live?'

Sharmila nodded. 'You know, I have this fascination for the place, but I never dared suggest to Deepak that we should go there. I'd love to see where he used to work, where it all happened. I've heard it's a beautiful city.'

'I'd love that. When Elspeth goes home I could always stay on for a couple of weeks.'

'Let's do it then,' said Sharmila beaming, holding her coffee cup up and, looking at her smiling eyes, Iris felt the warm rush of friendship, such as she hadn't felt with anyone since she and Sharmila had been together before.

Back at the Lake View Hotel, Iris knocked tentatively on Elspeth's door. It was late afternoon, and she was going to ask Elspeth to come to the bar for a conciliatory drink before dinner. She had to knock several times before she heard Elspeth shuffling over to the door.

'Oh, it's you,' Elspeth said pulling the door back. 'What do you want?'

'Please don't be cross with me, Elspeth. I know you're annoyed with me for going up to the hills, but it will only be for a few days, and it's very comfortable here.'

Then she stopped speaking. Behind Elspeth she spotted her suitcase open on the bed, her other bags ready packed on the floor.

'Why are you packing?'

'Because I'm going home. Back to England. It hasn't really worked out for us here, has it?'

'I'm sorry, Elspeth. Please don't go. I can postpone my trip for a while if you don't want me to go. I was thinking of staying on in India for a bit longer anyway. I could go then.'

Elspeth pursed her lips. 'No, my mind is made up. The hotel manager has already been in touch with the airline. There is a flight from Nagabhari to Delhi tomorrow morning which connects with a BA flight to London.'

'Oh, Elspeth. Look, I was going to ask you along to the bar for a drink so why don't you come along now. We can talk about this.'

'Alright. I suppose it can't do any harm and I could do with a drink. Let me get my stick.'

'Oh, you don't need that!' the words were out before Iris had time to think. Then she held her breath, waiting for Elspeth's angry reaction. But although Elspeth flushed, she quickly recovered herself. 'No, you're quite right. I won't take it.'

So, they walked along to the bar together and ordered gimlets, a club favourite in their day, and sat down at a window table to watch the sunset.

'I'm sorry things haven't worked out very well for us here, Elspeth,' Iris began. 'Perhaps we're just too different to have contemplated travelling together. We were very different when we were young, weren't we?'

Elspeth nodded. 'We were. Look, I know I've been difficult at times,' said Elspeth, 'And for that I'm sorry. I had forgotten how much bitterness I was harbouring, even after all these years.'

'Bitterness? But why, Elspeth? Why are you so bitter?'

Elspeth took a long sip of her gimlet, then toyed with her glass.

'I suppose I was jealous of you. That's why. And I'm still jealous of you.'

'But why? What was there to be jealous about?'

Elspeth took another sip of her drink and Iris was shocked to see tears in her eyes.

'You know, in 1943 I fell in love with a young man who used to come to the club. He wasn't my usual type and when I first saw him, I despised him just as everyone else did. The others used to laugh and joke about him. He wasn't one of our set, or even one of our class. Mummy would have been horrified if she'd known about it. He had very humble beginnings, but he had worked hard to get where he was.'

'Elspeth!' Iris breathed, the truth beginning to dawn on her.

'We got talking one day when I arrived before the rest of my friends, and I began to see that he was an interesting, caring person. We actually got on very well. So, I used to go to the club early on purpose to see him. He always used to go there after his afternoon shift at the hospital. We were getting on very well, and I thought something might actually come of it.'

'I had no idea that you were fond of Nigel,' Iris murmured.

'Then, something happened, and he stopped coming early to the club. Or if he came, he tried to avoid me. I found out afterwards that *you* had started volunteering at the hospital and that he'd fallen head over heels for you. One of the nurses told me. There was nothing I could do about it. Nothing.'

'Oh, Elspeth. I'm so, so sorry.'

'And then you met that other man, Edward Stark. Nigel started coming back to the club and we had a couple of conversations again. I thought there might be another chance for me. That didn't last long, though. He told me he had volunteered to go and work in a field hospital up at Imphal near the front. Then I found out that you were going too. He only volunteered to go because of you. Iris.'

Elspeth looked into Iris' eyes and Iris was shocked to see that tears were rolling down Elspeth's cheeks now. Her lips were trembling.

'He only went because of you, and he only died because of you, Iris. That's why I'm angry with you. I've never forgiven you. Because of you, I've never been happy.'

'I'm so, so, sorry, Elspeth. I've never got over the guilt of Nigel's death, myself. The fact that he died and I survived has haunted me my whole life. But I had no idea...'

'All the joy went out of life for me after that,' Elspeth went on. 'I just went through the motions of the daily routine until we came back to England. The office, the club, where I used to gossip and drink too much like my mother, and yours, but my heart wasn't in it. And then, when we got back to England, I married the first vaguely suitable man who happened to take an interest in me. Although I found out quite quickly that he wasn't even vaguely suitable.'

Iris was silent, she had no idea what she could say or do to make Elspeth feel better. Elspeth took another sip of gimlet and began speaking again.

'This trip has taught me a lot, though. It has shown me how little I knew of the real India when I lived here. We used to go about in our own little privileged bubble. We lived a life of luxury and idleness at the expense of others. All the time I've been away, I've looked back at it fondly, but coming back here has shown me how hollow our existence was here. All the time the real India went on without me even noticing it; the heat, the poverty, the inequality. And now I've come back, I've seen it for myself. It's as if I've never been here before. It's really opened my eyes.'

'I know what you mean, Elspeth.'

'I'm glad I've visited, but I have no desire to come back again. It has shown me a lot about India and a lot about myself. And it has also shown me that, for all your standoffishness in the old days, you were really no different to any of us. You were just trying to make your way in the world like we all were. I shouldn't have been jealous of you all these years.'

Iris sipped her drink and thought about what Elspeth had said.

'You know, now we've started to be honest with one another, it's such a shame that you're leaving. Won't you think again? I'm happy to postpone my trip into the hills. I've waited more than forty years, it won't hurt to wait another couple of weeks.'

Elspeth shook her head. 'As I said before, my mind is made up. It has been an interesting few weeks, but I've had enough. I need to go home.'

'Alright, but could I ask you to leave me one thing?'

Elspeth laughed. 'Whatever could you possibly want of mine? All my clothes are far too big for you. Not to mention old-fashioned.'

'Your stick,' Iris replied. 'The guide said I would need one in the hills but I couldn't find one in the bazaar, and it suddenly occurred to me that you might not be needing yours anymore.'

Elspeth laughed for a long time and dried her eyes on a tissue. It was the first time Iris had heard her laugh properly all the time they'd been travelling together.

'I have to hand it to you, Iris Grey, you have the cheek of the devil,' Elspeth said, 'but I suppose I owe it to you after what we've been through together. It will mean you won't be able to get away from me when you're up there in the hills, though. Every time you look at it, it will remind you of me.'

'That's not such a bad thing, Elspeth,' Iris smiled. 'It's not such a bad thing at all.'

23

Nagabhari, India, 1985

The next morning, Iris got up early to share a coffee with Elspeth and to see her off. The black and yellow taxi came at six o'clock, its headlights lighting up the gravel drive and the hotel steps, myriad insects dancing in the beams. Elspeth walked to the taxi unaided, carrying a bag, while the hotel porter loaded her suitcase into the boot. The taxi driver held the back door open.

Iris had thought that the goodbye would be awkward, but as they reached the taxi, Elspeth turned and put her arms around Iris and drew her close in a tight hug. After a moment's surprise, Iris returned the hug gladly.

'Goodbye Iris. I wish you well for your trip,' Elspeth said warmly. 'Do get in touch when you get back to England. I want to know how it all goes.'

'Of course. Thank you, Elspeth. Have a safe journey.'

'I'm actually glad I came,' Elspeth said, getting into the taxi.

'Me too. I think we both made a little progress.'

'We did that.' Elspeth patted her leg and winked.

Iris closed the taxi door with a smile and waved until the taillights of the taxi had disappeared along the lakeside road. She turned to go back into the hotel with a heavy heart. She felt guilty that she and Elspeth hadn't been able to confront their differences until it was too late to salvage their trip. But on the other hand, she was glad that they'd finally been able to be honest with one another.

She went into the dining room alone and ate an early breakfast as the sun rose over the lake. She watched the beauty unfold as the water and the distant palace turned from grey to pink to deep-red, and remembered once again how she'd loved to watch the sunrise over the lake as a girl. She had to tear herself away from the window to go back to her room to make the final preparations for her trek.

Mengu came for her at seven o'clock sharp. He was driven by an old man in a battered Land Rover. Iris had negotiated with the hotel to leave her suitcase and a couple of bags in the luggage store there, so all she had was a knapsack, together with Elspeth's walking stick, of course. Into the knapsack she'd packed some basic essentials for the next few days, her water-proofs, her spare clothes and toiletries. She was wearing her new boots that felt a little stiff and heavy.

She'd also packed three precious items to help her in her search; her 1944 diary, which she'd continued reading on and off all week, and the broken army badge that Gokal had given her. She'd wrapped that in tissue and put it in an inside pocket for safekeeping, but each time she'd handled it, it had given her a feeling of connection to Edward and to the past. And there was also Edward's photograph. The one he'd given her on the day they parted. It still made her heart twist with regret as she looked at the fading image; his earnest smile and the gentle look in his eyes.

'Good morning, Mrs Grey!' Mengu's smile lit up the grey dawn. He helped her into the back seat of the Land Rover. 'We will drive as far as the road will take us. That will take two to three hours. Then we must start walking.'

Mengu explained that the driver spoke no English, but that he was a safe pair of hands and knew the mountain roads well. The old man smiled broadly at Iris as she settled into the back.

They set off along the bumpy track beside the lake, then joined the metalled road at the junction. From there they made their way around the outskirts of the old British quarter and out of Nagabhari, soon leaving the town far behind them and heading west across the plain towards the hills. It was the same road that Edward had driven Iris out to the caves on and the one she and Elspeth had travelled only a couple of days before. She recalled with shame the way Elspeth had spoken to the guide, hoping that Mengu didn't know about it. But then she did her best to put that memory aside. There was no point dwelling on something she couldn't do anything about. Instead, she wondered if this was the way Edward and his companions had set out towards Nangtek in 1944. She realised that she hadn't been any further than the caves on this road before. When she'd gone into the hills in 1944 it had been by aircraft.

Soon they passed the entrance to the caves and the road wound on and up through forests and pastures, and past mountain lakes that shimmered in the morning sunlight. Looking back down the mountainside, Iris saw row upon row of terraced rice paddies, their surface reflecting the sun like glass. They passed slowly on through a couple of villages where rows of one-storey shops and dwellings straddled the road and people stared as they passed. Cattle and chickens wandered on the road and dogs barked at the vehicle and chased after it for a little way. These weren't Naga villages, Mengu explained. Those were still higher up and deeper into the hills.

The road wound on upwards, through wild, forested countryside. The road itself seemed as though it had recently been hewn out of the mountainside; it was flanked by an exposed, red earth bank, but Mengu said that it had been here since the war. The road surface was no longer tarmacked. Instead it was bumpy and rutted, and in places narrowed to a single lane. The driver had to slow right down on these sections and the Land Rover bucked and rocked its way through.

They travelled on along a steep mountainside between fields of ragged banana palms. Far below, a slow, wide river snaked its way along the valley bottom. There was no sign of habitation here and Iris realised that there hadn't been for miles. Staring out of the window at the endless landscape, row upon row of jungle-covered hills fading into the mist, Iris had a sense of just how remote this place was from the rest of the world. It came home to her again how hard it must have been to fight a war in this terrain.

At last, they reached the end of the road. The driver stopped the Land Rover and switched off the engine.

'This is it,' said Mengu. 'We walk from here. Are you ready, Mrs Grey?'

'Of course. I'm looking forward to it. But please call me Iris, if you don't mind, Mengu.'

Mengu spoke to the driver who turned the Land Rover round and drove away. That surprised Iris. For some reason she hadn't envisaged that happening. As she watched it disappearing round a bend in the road, she felt a sudden panic of abandonment, realising again just how remote this place was and how much she was in Mengu's hands.

'He will come back to this place in the morning in six days' time,' Mengu explained. 'That gives us three days to get to Ejeirong district. The weather is clear so I think we will make it. Alright, let's go!'

He hoisted his huge pack onto his shoulders and set off on a narrow path that led into the trees. As well as two tents he was carrying their bedding and cooking equipment. Iris followed and soon they were enveloped in the forest. It was so dense that fronds of giant ferns brushed them as they passed. Peering in between the trees, the canopy was so thick and high above them that the interior was dark.

They walked on like that for an hour or so, the only sound the crackle of their feet on the jungle floor, the hum of insects and the whirring of cicadas, occasionally the whoop of a monkey from deep within the trees. As she walked, Iris got a sense of the vastness of the jungle; dense, evergreen rainforest stretching for miles on either side of them. The vegetation was all the same: giant ferns, clumps of towering bamboo, majestic teak trees. How easy it would be to get lost without a guide. She thought about Edward and his companions. Had they walked this way? Had they had a guide too? They crossed a fast-flowing stream that ran between smooth boulders where Mengu stooped to fill up their water bottles.

'It's alright,' he said with a broad smile when he caught Iris eyeing the bottles suspiciously. 'I will boil the water before we drink it. I don't want to get sick either.'

They reached a grassy clearing after an hour or so where Mengu suggested they should stop for lunch. He spread a groundsheet out for Iris to sit on and produced some chapatis and fried rice.

'We will have to make a fire and cook this evening, but I brought these from home for now.'

Iris accepted gratefully and began to eat, realising how

hungry the walk had made her. 'Why is this clearing here?' she asked. 'Does someone want to farm it?'

Mengu shook his head and laughed. 'It is wild boar. They have destroyed this area. It was mostly bamboo before. But don't worry. They have eaten all the bamboo and moved on.'

In the afternoon they walked for another three or four hours. Although it was impossible to see the sun, the atmosphere was hot and steamy and Iris was beginning to flag. When they reached another small stream, Mengu said, 'We will set up camp here for tonight. It is too far to the first village to get there today, we will stay there tomorrow night.'

Iris helped Mengu to pitch the two small tents on the rough ground, pulling the guy ropes tight, hammering the pegs into the soil. She felt a tingle of excitement at the prospect of sleeping out here in the jungle, miles from civilisation. She hadn't camped for thirty years or so, not since her children were small, but a luxurious and well-equipped frame tent on a campsite in the South of France hardly counted as camping compared to this.

Mengu lit a fire and from the pockets of his backpack produced some slivers of meat, onions, peppers and a packet of rice. On a single pan over the flames, he cooked up some very passable and tasty fried rice. The light was fading fast as they sat on the groundsheet to eat the meal. Iris watched Mengu as he tucked in. She wondered how he came to straddle the two worlds of modern India and hilltribe village. The two were perfectly reflected in the way he dressed.

'Do you come from one of the villages originally?' she asked tentatively.

'Yes. I was born in 1939 in a village near Kohima. It was a Naga village, very traditional, completely cut off from the outside world.'

'So how did you come to be guiding tourists in Nagabhari?' she asked.

In the half-light his face looked suddenly serious and Iris began to regret her question, but then he began to speak.

'My village was very near the fighting in 1944. We could hear the shelling and the gunfire. Sometimes stray bombs would fall in the forest near us. Trees would come crashing down, fires would destroy large areas of jungle. People in the village were terrified. Nothing like that had ever happened before, but there was nowhere to go. Then one day a bomb hit our village. No one even knew if it was Japanese or British. Many people were killed and some of the homes were destroyed. Our home was one of them. My father and mother both died.'

'Oh, how terrible, Mengu,' Iris said, shocked.

'Yes, it was. So many terrible things happened in the war. Although the elders of the village would have happily given me a home and looked after me, some missionaries came to the village soon afterwards and took all those children who'd lost their parents in the bombing down to an orphanage in Nagabhari. That's where I grew up and went to school. I learned English there too. So, you see, I'm Naga but I'm also Indian too,' he smiled his wide smile.

'That's fascinating. I knew there was an orphanage in Nagabhari, but I had no idea there were Naga children there.'

'It was a good place to grow up. The missionaries were kind. But you see, when people come here and want to go into the hills to see where the Burma campaign was fought or to find out what the conditions were like, I'm more than happy to take them. It is part of my history too.'

'I'm wondering if you might know something about this badge,' she said on an impulse, fishing in her bag for the rusty object. She unwrapped it and showed it to him. He produced a small torch and examined it carefully under the light, turning it over and over in his fingers. Then he shook his head and handed it back to her.

'It is a military badge. A cap badge probably, but I'm sorry, I don't know which regiment. Some of the older people in the villages might know though, some of them had quite a bit of contact with the British soldiers during the campaign.'

When the light faded, Iris snuggled down inside her tent in the sleeping bag Mengu had given her. Although she was exhausted from the day's exertions, sleep wouldn't come. The sound of insects was amplified in the stillness of the night and it was difficult to shut it out. She couldn't stop thinking about Mengu's village; of children running in terror, screaming when the bombs hit. Then her mind returned to the hospital camp. The sound of insects became shelling and gunfire in her confused, exhausted mind and soon she was back there again with Nigel near Kohima under that tree with machine-gun fire raining down on her.

In the morning she woke early and could hear Mengu moving around, lighting a fire and fetching water from the stream. By the time she'd pulled on her clothes and emerged from the tent, he had already brewed her a cup of tea and made porridge in the pan. After they'd eaten breakfast and packed up the camp, they set off once again on the path that led them deeper into the hills. They walked for hours under a burning sun and reached the first signs of habitation late in the morning.

'This is Nangtek village,' Mengu said as they stepped out from the edge of the forest at the top of a hill and looked down on the wooden roofs of a group of houses. They clambered down the hill towards the village and were soon walking down what looked like the main street. It was lined with rickety houses made of wood and bamboo. Most were single-storey, but the upper floors of the two-storey houses overhung the road. People sat in front of their homes, or hovered shyly in the shade of the eaves, eyeing the strangers. Women and girls carried babies in sarongs on their backs.

Firewood was stacked against the front walls of all the houses and in some of them they caught glimpses of women weaving cloth by hand on great looms.

Eventually they came to a wide-open space that looked like a village square – a flat area of bare earth surrounded by low buildings. On one side was a rickety shed-like structure that looked like the village shop. It was really no more than a kiosk with a hatch in the front, the wooden flap held up with string. Iris' heart leapt when she caught sight of the faded words "Post Office" painted along the top of the building.

'Can I speak to the people in that shop?' she asked. Mengu nodded and they approached the building. An old couple sat behind the counter chatting together; the old man was smoking a cheroot. They looked up and smiled their welcome with blackened teeth. The shelves inside the shop were stacked with packets of bidis, faded tins of fruit and vegetables, bags of several types of nut, bunches of tiny bananas. Three plucked chickens hung by their necks from the ceiling. Mengu bowed to the old couple and said some words of greeting, then he asked Iris what she wanted to ask them.

'Could you ask if they were here during the war, and if so, if they remember this man coming to collect mail?'

She took the photograph of Edward from her pocket and Mengu handed it to the old couple who puzzled over it for a while, frowning, while Mengu spoke to them. The two conferred together for a while, the old man scratching his bald head, then he handed the photograph back and replied to Mengu.

'He says that many British men came through the village

during the war. This old building was a post office then, although it isn't any longer. Post used to come in by mule via Imphal and Kohima in those days. He doesn't remember this man in particular, though. It is far too long ago. But he says we should go along to the headman's house and ask there. The headman is old and remembers the war very well.'

By this time a crowd of small children had gathered around the shop, staring at the newcomers with huge, curious eyes. On hearing what the old man said, one of the little girls took Iris' hand and guided her, followed by Mengu and the rest of the crowd, through a maze of wooden huts where skinny cattle wandered, and pigs and chickens rooted between the buildings. They arrived at a large, square structure, made of planks of rough wood like all the rest but with a thatched roof. On the front wall dozens of buffalo skulls were on display.

The headman came to the door, smoking a long pipe. He was tall and imposing, dressed in a sarong and a wool blanket. He smiled broadly and greeted Iris and Mengu by putting his hands together and bowing his head. They both returned the gesture, then Mengu stepped forward and spoke to him, no doubt explaining their mission. The headman's eyes lit up with interest and he gestured for them to come inside his house. The children melted away and Iris followed Mengu up a couple of wooden steps and into the smoky interior. She looked around the room, her eyes adjusting to the gloom. The house appeared to consist of one main chamber built around a central open fire which had been made on slabs of stone. Smoke curled upwards through the open room and out through a hole in the ceiling.

There was no one else inside the house, except a bent old woman in the corner, sieving rice in a raffia pan. There were wooden benches all around the walls though, so it was clearly some sort of gathering place. The old man beckoned them forward and offered them stools beside the fire. Although it was cooler outside now at this altitude, it felt extremely hot beside the fire and Iris was soon perspiring heavily. The headman said something to the old woman, who came forward, smiling and put a huge cast iron kettle on the fire.

'I have told him about your quest,' Mengu said, leaning towards Iris. 'He would like to see your photograph.'

She took it out of her pocket once again and handed it to the headman. He wandered over to the door with it and studied it in the light of the sun. When he turned round, Iris could tell from his expression that he didn't recognise Edward. He returned to the fire shaking his head.

The old woman made tea in earthenware cups and handed them round, then retreated to her corner.

'I'm sorry, he doesn't remember the man in the picture,' Mengu said. 'Why don't you show him the badge? He does remember that many soldiers passed through this village during the Burma campaign. Some of them even camped here overnight.'

Once again, the old man took the badge over to the light and looked at it carefully. This time, when he turned round his expression was different. He was smiling. He returned to the fireside and spoke to Mengu. There was excitement in his tone. Iris waited with bated breath until he'd finished speaking.

Mengu said, 'He thinks the "Force" on the badge stands for "V-Force". Have you heard of them? He says they were a special, secret force that went behind enemy lines. Their job was to harass the enemy and gather intelligence about their movements.'

Iris thought long and hard. It did ring a bell. A very dim and distant one, though. Then it came back to her. She recalled Doctor Bourne telling her that V-Force were the army's eyes and ears on the ground in the Naga Hills. She remembered him tapping the side of his nose to indicate how secret the organisation was, and saying that they were incredibly brave. Then she remembered something else; the tall man slipping between the trees to speak to some officers and hand them some papers. It had surprised her that he hadn't been dressed like a soldier, but in a billowing white shirt.

Had Edward been a member of V-Force? Had he been one of those extraordinary men brave enough to go behind enemy lines to harass them and disrupt their plans? She smiled proudly, thinking of the quiet courage in his gentle eyes and how he'd kept his secret from her so that it was only now and by going to these lengths that she was finally finding out the truth.

The headman was still talking to Mengu. Finally he turned to her and translated. 'He says that some V-Force men came this way, but they were mostly working in villages in Ejeirong province. He doesn't know what they were doing there, but if you go and ask the headmen in the villages there, they will tell you what they know.'

They were asked to stay in the headman's house that night. In the evening, after a delicious stew of wild boar and rice, the men of the village treated them to a display of traditional dancing in the village square. As Iris sat in pride of place on the edge of the square, surrounded by the village children, watching the torchlight glinting on the moving bodies and listening to the chanting and the mournful moan of the pipe music, she wondered if Edward and his friends had also been entertained like this all those years ago.

24

Naga Hills, India, 1985

Early the next morning they left the village of Nangtek behind them and walked on through the rainforest towards Ejeirong province. The villagers had pressed gifts upon them as they left: fruit and cured meats, cigarettes and nuts for their travels. They had garlanded them with necklaces of marigold and made them promise to go back on their return journey.

These forested hills felt even more remote than those they'd walked the previous day and the path was even less distinct. The jungle was thicker and more impenetrable here, the trunks of the tall trees strangled by rope-like creepers interspersed with giant ferns, palm bushes and bamboo. Iris wondered how Mengu knew the way but she didn't want him to suspect she didn't trust him, so she kept quiet. Here, where the ground was rough and slippery, she was glad of Elspeth's stick. She leaned on it to help her climb and to stop her from falling over through muddy patches. Using the stick made her think of Elspeth. Where would she be now? Back home in

Cheltenham, her family around her? How would she explain to them that she no longer needed her stick? And would she be reflecting on her journey and what it had taught her? Iris was sure she would, and realised that she was actually looking forward to meeting Elspeth again on her return to England and telling her all about her extraordinary trip into the Naga Hills.

They walked for hours until they came to the first settlement. This was just a few huts, not really a village at all. It lacked the prosperity and buzz of Nangtek. The headman greeted them politely, but shook his head when Iris showed him the badge and the photograph of Edward. They quickly moved on, back into the forest, climbing higher and higher between the trees, going deeper and deeper into the hills towards the Burmese border. Every couple of hours they came to another village and once again would take out the photograph and the badge. And every time the headman would examine it carefully and return it shaking his head.

'Are we in Ejeirong district now?' she asked and Mengu nodded.

'These villages are very remote as you see. The villagers rarely see strangers and like to keep to themselves.'

They ate their lunch on a hilltop in a clearing with a breath-taking view, overlooking layer upon layer of hills that faded away into the blue mist. Lunch consisted of hard-boiled eggs and unleavened bread that the Nangtek villagers had pressed upon them. After they'd eaten their fill, they pushed on still further into the forest. Iris was beginning to despair of ever finding anything out about Edward. The deeper she went into the jungle, the gloomier she felt. What a fool she'd been to even hope that this journey might be fruitful. She began to prepare herself for the inevitable point at which they would have to turn round and retrace their steps to Nagabhari empty-handed.

They reached the remote village of Langchong halfway through the afternoon. It clung to the edge of the hillside, overlooking a deep, rocky ravine through which a torrent thundered, hundreds of feet below. It was a much bigger community than any they had passed through before that day and Iris' spirits lifted as they walked down the main thoroughfare, past a street market where fruit, vegetables and live chickens and ducks were on sale. They ended up in the main square. There was a huge peepul tree in the centre where old men sat on benches in the shade smoking and gossiping. Mengu approached them and Iris watched as he introduced himself and began to engage the old men in conversation. She smiled, reflecting on how lucky she'd been to have found him by chance. He had such natural charm and enthusiasm, everyone warmed to him immediately.

In a few minutes he returned to her with one of the old gentlemen in tow. This man was dressed in a black tunic and carried a teak staff. He had long earrings made out of animal bones and wore leather gaiters on his bare legs. He smiled a toothless smile as he approached Iris.

'This is Kuki,' Mengu said. 'He is eighty years old and remembers the war years quite well. He will take us to the headman's house. The headman is a little younger, but together they may be able to help us.'

They walked through the streets with Kuki striding ahead. He was a striking figure, holding his staff, and people came out of their houses to stare, just as they had in Nangtek. The headman's house was more elaborate than the one in Nangtek. Again, it was built of wood, with thick thatch on the roof, but this house had two storeys, it was perched on the edge of the ravine and at the back was a terrace that looked straight out over the precipice. Instead of actual buffalo skulls, the outer walls were decorated with colourful paintings depicting them. The headman came out onto the front steps and greeted Kuki and Mengu, then he turned towards Iris and acknowledged her by putting his hands together and tipping his head forward in a bow. She responded by mirroring his greeting.

They went inside the house and as they entered, Iris was shocked to see a row of human skulls laid out on a shelf just inside the door. Mengu said, 'Do not worry, Iris, those are from a very long time ago. The Naga people no longer hunt heads. It has been banned for a hundred years or so.'

'Very reassuring,' she said quietly with a shudder and followed the others out to the porch that looked out over the ravine. Almost mechanically, she got out the picture of Edward and handed it to the headman. The headman took it reverentially and looked at it carefully for a few seconds, then gave it to Kuki. Then both men started speaking to Mengu at once. They were animated, gesticulating, pointing outside. Iris watched them carefully, trying to glean something of what was being said. Her heart was hammering. They knew something, she was sure of it.

'What are they saying?' she asked Mengu, unable to contain herself.

'Wait, please. I need to let them finish,' he replied. When the old men had stopped speaking, Mengu asked them some questions which they answered with some head-scratching and some hesitation. At last he turned back to Iris.

'They recognise the man in the picture.' Iris gasped and tears sprung to her eyes. 'Did they meet him? Do they know what happened to him?' she asked breathlessly.

'Yes, but you need to prepare yourself. I'm afraid it is not good news.'

She clung to the wooden rail on the edge of the balcony,

sensing the torrent far, far below. A dizzy feeling overcame her, and she staggered a little.

'Perhaps you had better come inside,' Mengu said, taking her arm. He guided her into the house and sat her down on a bench. An old woman brought her some liquid in a chipped glass. It smelled like alcohol.

'Drink please – it will do you good,' Mengu said. She put the glass to her lips and downed the sweet liquid that coursed down her throat like firewater. Immediately she felt her limbs go heavy.

'Tell me what they said, please, Mengu.'

He sat down beside her. 'I'm so sorry. This will be hard for you to hear. They say that the man in the photograph came here with some others in the spring of 1944. He came with two other Englishmen. They were all from V-Force. They also had six Ghurkha soldiers with them. They spoke the Naga language very well. Their mission was to recruit men from the village to become guerrillas to fight alongside them behind enemy lines against the Japanese. Their job would be to set fire to Japanese camps, to disrupt their advance in any way possible and report back any intelligence they discovered. Some of the younger men from the village agreed to join them. They were due to start out the next morning to a camp where they would be trained in guerrilla tactics.

'But in the evening, when everyone was seated around the fire eating and drinking, a Japanese patrol came out of the jungle and took them by surprise. They came from every direction. They must have been watching and waiting for the right moment. They surrounded them, dragged the Englishmen and the Ghurkhas off to the village square. There, they tied them up to each other in a line and killed them all one by one. Some were bayoneted, some were shot.'

Iris gasped. The shock of finally finding out the truth hit her hard. She stared at Mengu, unable to speak.

'The young men who had agreed to join them were lucky not to have been killed too, but the Japanese left them alone. Then they threw most of the bodies down the ravine, but the headman wouldn't let them take the body of your friend. He knew he was the leader and had liked him very much. So, he pleaded with the Japanese to let him bury him in the village. The villagers buried him in the shade of the peepul tree in the centre of the village. I'm so sorry, Iris.'

She felt him take her hand and she let the tears fall. After all these years, after this long, arduous journey, she suddenly felt utterly beaten. Edward, with his sweet smile and beautiful eyes had died, up here in this friendly but remote village. He had died a horrible, painful death. And all the while she'd waited day in, day out for the postman to bring her a love letter from him. She was angry with herself for doubting him.

She sat there, holding Mengu's hand, letting the news seep through her. He'd been incredibly brave, risking everything to work on this highly dangerous mission for V-Force. He'd paid the ultimate sacrifice. Iris realised that she could finally let the past rest, in the knowledge that Edward hadn't abandoned her. But the thought that he had died such a horrific death was hard to bear.

'Can we go and see his grave?' she asked when she was able to form words.

'Of course, but the headman has something to show you.'

She stood up and the headman was beckoning her into the building. She followed him up the wooden steps and into the dark interior. He was gesturing for her to come into a little storeroom at the back. She followed him inside. He was bending down, taking a black metal box from under a shelf. He opened it up and took out something and handed it to her.

It was a photograph of her as a young woman. She took it and looked at it. She was staring back at her young self; she looked pretty, tanned and with perfect white teeth, her blonde hair tumbling around her shoulders. How innocent she'd been then, how full of hope. The photo looked faded and old, dirty too. It was speckled with spots of dirt, but looking closer she realised that they weren't spots of dirt at all, they were spots of dried blood. Her hands began to shake.

'Come, come,' the headman said, smiling his toothless smile. He guided her out into the main hall and sat her down on a bench. She put the photograph down and he handed her some more things.

He said something to Mengu. 'These things were found on your friend's body. They kept them in case anyone ever came looking for him.'

The headman handed her two envelopes. Her heart missed a beat. The first had her own handwriting on the front and was addressed to Edward at the post office in Nangtek. It was the first letter she'd written to him. The second was addressed to her in Nagabhari, but bore no stamp. It was the letter she'd craved to receive, the letter she'd wondered about for forty years. She pulled it out of the envelope.

My dearest Iris,

Thank you for your letter which I collected from Nangtek PO this morning. I'm writing straight back but am not sure when I'll get the opportunity to post it. I am missing you so much, Iris, and can't wait to be with you again. I'm not sure when that will be, but it's what I'm craving most of all up here in the hills

Our mission is taking us deeper into the Naga Hills. The people are very friendly and welcome us wherever we go. I can't tell you exactly where we are going, there are aspects of this trip that are confidential, but I will keep in touch with you as best I can. I'm hoping that I will only be away for a few weeks, then we will be

*together again. This time I'm hoping that I won't be torn away
from you quite so quickly.*

*Do write to me again and tell me your news. I think about you
night and day and can't wait to take you in my arms again and tell
you in person how much I love you.*

Your ever loving

Edward

Iris read it again and again until the tears stopped her
from seeing the words. Aware of someone hovering over her,
she looked up and there was the headman standing in front of
her. He was waiting to give her something else. She held out
her hand and into it he put two small silver objects. They were
cufflinks. The ones she'd given Edward, engraved with their
initials intertwined. It touched her deeply that he'd carried
them with him, even on the day he died. She remembered his
face when she'd given them to him at the abandoned temple,
his eyes widening as he examined them.

'When you're ready,' Mengu was saying when she looked
up. 'We can go up to the peepul tree.'

She walked beside Mengu, behind the headman and Kuki,
back along the street towards the great peepul tree in the
village square. People watched shyly from their houses as the
solemn procession passed through.

When they reached the square, Iris noticed that the old
men had disappeared from the benches; perhaps they knew
the nature of her mission here. Had word spread already, or
had their instinct told them?

'It is here,' the headman said in stumbling English.

Behind the great tree trunk, in the shade of its spreading
branches, stood a tall, solid-looking stone. One word had been
carved into it in Naga script.

'What does it say?' she asked Mengu.

'It says "brave warrior",' he replied. 'Now we will leave you here, so you can be at peace.' He turned and walked away from the square with the headman and Kuki.

She thought about his words as the tears began to fall again. She knelt before the stone, aware that under the earth beneath her lay the man she had loved and missed for more than forty years. Would she now be at peace? She thought of his tender smile, the light in his gentle brown eyes, the way he had taken her in his arms and kissed her. He'd been here in this beautiful spot amongst these loving people deep in these remote mountains all this time. She was quite sure that he was at peace here, and now she knew that, she realised that she could go on with her life. That she could be at peace too.

THANK you for reading *The Lake Palace*. I hope you've enjoyed reading it as much as I enjoyed writing it!

I'd love to hear your feedback either through my Facebook page or my website (www.annbennettauthor.com) where you can sign up for news and updates about my books.

If you've enjoyed this book, you might also like to read my next book, *The Lake Pagoda,* a story of love, loss and survival set in French Indochina in the '30s and '40s. Please turn over to read an extract.

EXTRACT FROM THE LAKE PAGODA

Chapter 1

Paris, November 1946

Arielle pulled her shawl tightly around her shoulders and stepped out of the entrance to the apartment building and onto the broad pavement of Boulevard St Germaine. An icy wind whipped around her, driving up from the River Seine, funnelled by the tall buildings. She shivered and gritted her teeth against the weather. It was so alien to her, this biting cold air that chilled you to the marrow of your bones. In her native Hanoi, the temperature, even in the cooler months, was always comfortable and she was so used to the sultry heat of that city that this Paris winter was a cruel shock.

Even so, she needed to get out. She couldn't stay inside the stuffy, cramped apartment a moment longer, and while her father was sleeping it was difficult to do anything in that tiny space without disturbing him. So, each morning she left the building to tramp the streets of this alien city, exploring the alleys of the Latin Quarter, the cobbled lanes and churches of the île de la Cité, the boulevards and gardens of the Eighth Arondissement. And as she walked, she watched the stylish Parisians going about their business, dashing to and fro in fashionable clothes, getting out of taxis, riding on trams, pouring down the steps of the metro. She was trying to understand her new home, to find her place in it, to find some meaningful connection with this great, intimidating city. And there was something else she was searching for too.

Now, as she braced herself against the wind and started walking along the boulevard away from the apartment, she glanced guiltily back up at the windows on the third floor. She always worried when she left Papa alone. What if he were to wake up and call out for her? What if he had one of his coughing fits? But he always encouraged her to go. 'Go on, explore while I'm resting. You need to get to know the place. You can't stay cooped up with a sick old man all day. I'll be fine on my own.' But still she worried.

She carried on down the road, making for the market in Rue Mouffetard. Cars and buses crawled past belting out fumes. Through the lines of slow-moving traffic wove bicycles and pony traps, army jeeps too. It felt so bleak here and so dull after the vibrant colours of Hanoi; the plane trees that lined the pavements had lost their leaves, their branches stark against the tall, pale buildings, and the sky between them was an ominous slate grey.

She walked past a couple of bus stops without pausing. She'd never yet got on a bus in Paris; she had no idea how they worked and was afraid of drawing attention to herself, even though she told herself it was perfectly safe here to do so. Years of having to keep a low profile in Hanoi had made her fearful of attention from anyone. Not that she need worry here in Paris, people barely noticed her. She could walk in the midst of a crowd as if she didn't exist. And if anyone's eyes did happen to light on her, seeing her dark skin and black hair they would quickly flick away, for she was half Vietnamese and it was as if she were invisible to them; a nobody.

She turned off the main road and walked towards the Jardins du Luxembourg. She loved these beautiful gardens with their wide-open lawns, broad sweeping paths and the elegant palace that dominated the centre. It reminded her of the gracious French colonial buildings of Hanoi; the Opera House, the Palais du Gouvernement, the Metropole Hotel. Despite the biting cold she would sometimes come here to sit on a bench and stare at the beautiful building; half-closing her eyes she could dream she was back home. But today there was no time. She needed to get to the market and back home before her father needed her.

Putting her head down against the biting wind, she hurried on and soon reached Rue Mouffetard where the market was in full swing, stalls piled high with fruit and vegetables. Despite the post-war rationing, stallholders at this market were adept at obtaining supplies; autumn fruits – apples and pears were piled up on one stall, potatoes and greens on another, yet another was selling whole, plucked chickens and another cheeses from the countryside, oozing and ripe. Arielle went from stall to stall buying what she and her father needed for the next couple of days. It reminded her a little of Hang Be market in the centre of Hanoi, where she used to buy food for the two of them until the war had swept that easy life away. But here there was no exotic fruit or plump, luscious seafood. There was no bartering either and she had to restrain herself from asking for a better price for a kilo of apples or a litre of unpasteurised milk. The stallholders dealt with her stiffly, unsmilingly and sometimes with suspicion, and as she turned away she could sense them whispering about her. It made her feel small, isolated, and a long way from home, but she knew there was nothing she could do about it.

It began to rain as she crossed the cobbles of a little square and carried on into the Rue Descartes. Her shopping bag was heavy now, loaded with produce. It dragged on her shoulder, but it was still quite a way back to the Boulevard St Germaine. She wrapped her shawl more tightly around her, shivering in the chill winter air and looked around for somewhere to shelter until the shower had passed. A bar-brasserie loomed up ahead where the pavement widened out at a junction. It had a red-painted awning above the door. Perhaps she could stand under there for a few minutes? She was far too timid to even think about going inside.

When she reached the building, she sidled underneath the porch and glanced in through the steamed-up window, taking in the polished tables, the elaborate glass and marble bar, the rows of bottles stacked on the shelves behind it. It was just after noon and a rowdy lunchtime crowd was propping up the bar, laughing and joking, calling for more drinks. Arielle saw instantly that they were soldiers. She peered at their khaki uniforms, the dark caps they were wearing. Someone pushed open the door and left, walking quickly away from Arielle along Rue de Montagne, but before the door slammed shut, she caught a burst of conversation and her heart beat faster. The men were speaking English. They must be American GIs, still stationed in Paris after the end of the war, waiting for their transport home.

Her interest piqued, she leaned even closer to the window and stared inside, her hot breath clouding the glass. She was searching for something, someone. She scanned the faces, many contorted in exaggerated laughter, flushed with alcohol, but none were familiar. Then one man turned round and her heart leapt as she caught a flash of tawny hair. Could that be him? She looked closer, not even able to blink, but as he turned towards the window momentarily, she was quickly disappointed. The face was unfamiliar and the hair wasn't quite the shade of flaming red she was looking for. She shrunk back against the wall. The man she was looking for couldn't possibly be here in Paris, she reasoned. If he were here, he would surely have been in touch with her.

Suddenly she wanted to be away from the noisy bar. She was glad when the rain eased off after a few minutes. Leaving the shelter of the porch, she shouldered her bag and carried on, along Rue de la Montagne and Rue St Genevieve, eventually emerging onto the wide pavements of the Boulevard St Germaine.

The concierge was standing in the doorway to her apartment, hands on hips as Arielle entered the hallway.

'Bonjour, madame,' Arielle said with a polite smile, but the woman just nodded curtly and turned away. With a sigh Arielle started the long walk up the steep stairs to the apartment.

Her father was sitting up in bed and as always she was shocked by how gaunt and pale he looked. His lined face was almost grey in the pale light.

'Are you alright, Papa?' She heaved the bag off her shoulder and went to his bedside to peck him on the cheek.

'Of course. How was your walk?'

'It was good,' she said brightly, not wanting to tell him how people shunned and ignored her. 'I bought fruit and cheese, some baguettes, oh and a chicken for supper.'

'You're a good girl,' he said, holding out a bony hand. 'I'm so lucky to have you.'

'Oh, Papa. Nonsense. I'm glad to be here.'

She went into the kitchenette to brew some tea. It was a

tiny, windowless room, little more than a cupboard. The whole apartment was small, even though it was in a gracious building with high ceilings and floor-length windows. Her father's cousin had allowed them to stay there when they'd arrived, penniless from Hanoi a few months before. He'd only visited once, to give them a key and show them around, before retreating to his large house in Neuilly.

'The last tenants left it in a bit of a state...' It was true. They hadn't even washed up from their last meal and their dirty sheets were still on the beds, but even though she was dropping with exhaustion from the journey, Arielle had got to work straight away, washing and scrubbing, dusting the surfaces and cleaning the floors.

Now, she took the tea out to Papa and handed it to him, noticing how his hands shook nowadays. She forced herself to smile but inside she couldn't stop anxious thoughts from surfacing. He was fading before her very eyes. All those weeks on the ship from Haiphong, rolling around on the high seas had taken its toll, lying on a bunk in a cramped cabin, too sick to get out for fresh air. And the terrible months before that locked up in the Citadel. She shivered to think of them now. It was good to put them behind her, but they had left their mark on her father, for sure.

'Will you sit with me and have your tea, Arielle?' Papa asked with pleading eyes.

She shook her head. 'In a few minutes, Papa. I need to get the soup on for lunch first.'

She went back into the kitchenette and peeled onions, potatoes, garlic, leeks and carrots, sweated them in butter in a saucepan over the flickering gas flame. Then she added stock and water and left it to simmer. Wiping her hands, she slipped into her bedroom. It was hardly big enough to qualify as a room, just wide enough for a single bed. There, she felt in her top drawer for the picture. It was hidden under her underwear. She wasn't sure why, but she didn't want Papa to look at it. Perhaps the memories it held for her were too precious to share? She drew it out and placed it on the end of the bed so she could look at it in the weak light from the window. It was a charcoal sketch of the Tran Quoc Pagoda on the West Lake, Hanoi, its many tiered roofs reaching to the sky. It stood proudly on its promontory, surrounded by palm trees, its reflection clear in the still waters of the lake. Just looking at it took her back there, to where so much had happened to her over the years. She could almost feel the sultry air of that city wrap itself around her as she stared at the sketch. And as she looked, the past became real and it was as if he was beside her again, his arms around her, and when she turned to smile at him he kissed her on the lips.

ACKNOWLEDGMENTS

Special thanks go to my friend and writing buddy Siobhan Daiko for her constant support and encouragement over the past ten years. To Rafa and Xavier at Cover Kitchen for their wonderful cover design; to Johnny Hudspith and Trenda Lundin for their inspirational editing, to my sisters, for reading and commenting on early drafts, and to everyone who's supported me down the years by reading my books.

ABOUT THE AUTHOR

Ann Bennett was born in Pury End, a small village in Northamptonshire and now lives in Surrey. *The Lake Palace* is her tenth novel. Her first book, *Bamboo Heart: A Daughter's Quest*, was inspired by her father's experience as a prisoner of war on the Thai-Burma Railway. *Bamboo Island: The Planter's Wife*, *A Daughter's Promise*, *Bamboo Road: The Homecoming*, *The Tea Planter's Club* and *The Amulet* are also about WWII in South East Asia. Together they form the Echoes of Empire collection.

She has also written *The Lake Pavilion* a novel set in British India in the 1930s to which *The Lake Palace* is a follow-up, *The Lake Pagoda* and *The Lake Villa*, both set in French Indochina during WWII. Ann's other books, *The Runaway Sisters*, bestselling *The Orphan House*, *The Child Without a Home* and *The Forgotten Children* are published by Bookouture.

Ann is married with three grown up sons and a granddaughter and works as a lawyer.

For more details please visit www.annbennettauthor.com

ALSO BY ANN BENNETT

Bamboo Heart: A Daughter's Quest

Bamboo Island: The Planter's Wife

Bamboo Road: The Homecoming

A Daughter's Promise

The Tea Planter's Club

The Amulet

The Lake Pavilion

The Lake Pagoda

The Lake Villa

The Child Without a Home

The Forgotten Children

The Orphan House

The Runaway Sisters

Printed in Great Britain
by Amazon